SELECTED STORIES

James Kelman

6

CANONGATE POCKET CLASSICS

First published as a Pocket Classic in 2001 by
Canongate Books Ltd, 14 High Street, Edinburgh
EHI ITE.

'The Bevel' and 'The Hitchhiker' first published by
Polygon 1983; copyright © James Kelman 1983.

'Pictures' and 'Lassies are trained that way' first
published by Secker & Warburg 1991; copyright ©
James Kelman 1991.

'Old Francis' and 'In with the doctor' first published by Secker & Warburg 1987; copyright ©
James Kelman 1987.

10 9 8 7 6 5 4 3 2 1

The publishers gratefully acknowledge general sub-
sidy from the Scottish Arts Council towards the
Canongate Classics and Pocket Classics series.

Typeset in 10pt Plantin by Palimpsest Book
Production Limited, Polmont, Stirlingshire.

Printed and bound by Omnia Books, Glasgow.

CANONGATE CLASSICS
Series Editor: Roderick Watson
Editorial Board: John Pick, Cairns Craig,
Dorothy McMillan

British Library Cataloguing-in-Publication Data
A catalogue record for this volume is available
on request from the British Library.

ISBN I 84195 159 5

www.canongate.net

SELECTED STORIES

JAMES KELMAN

James Kelman was born in Glasgow in 1946. His early employment included a variety of manual and semi-skilled jobs, ranging from farm worker to bus driver. In 1973 his first collection of stories, *An Old Pub Near the Angel*, was published in Maine, USA. This was followed in 1976 by *Three Glasgow Writers* (with Tom Leonard and Alex Hamilton) and a now rare booklet, *Short Tales from the Nightshift* (1978).

As with the poetry of Tom Leonard, Kelman's prose fiction has been influential among young writers, using language perhaps as a counter to the prevalence of middle and upper-middle-class mores and values in standard English literary form. He achieved wide critical success with the publication of *Not Not While the Giro, and other stories* (1983) and *The Busconductor Hines* (1984). These books were followed in 1985 by *Lean Tales* (with Agnes Owens and Alasdair Gray), and *A Chancer*. His short story collection *Greyhound for Breakfast* won the 1987 Cheltenham Prize, while in 1989 his novel *A Disaffection* was awarded the James Tait Black Memorial Prize. The short stories of *The Burn* (1991) won a Scottish Arts Council Award and his 1994 novel *How late it was, how late* received both the Booker Prize and The Writers

Guild award for Best Fiction Book. For the 1999 short story collection *The Good Times* he shared the Stakis Prize for Scottish Writer of the Year, and also received the 1999 Spirit of Scotland Award for writers.

The Busconductor Hines and *A Disaffection* have been translated into French while other works have been translated into German, Dutch, Norwegian and Spanish.

Kelman has also written a number of plays for the theatre including *The Busker*, *In the Night* and *One, two – hey!* while *Hardie and Baird & Other Plays* was published in 1991 and in 1998 *The Art of the Big Bass Drum* was broadcasted by BBC Radio 3. A collection of his essays was published as *Some Recent Attacks: Essays Cultural and Political* (1992).

The Bevel

WHEN I WOKE up the sun was already quite strong and it was clammy in the caravan; also it seemed like the midges had started biting. I had to rise. Chas was snoring in his bunk but in the other there was neither sound nor movement amongst the big heap of blankets. I gave up worrying about that a few days earlier. I struck a match and lit a cigarette. Time to get up: I shouted.

Chas moved; he blinked then muttered unintelligibly. I told him it was going to be another scorcher. He nodded. He peered at the big heap of blankets and raised a foot and let it crash down. An arm reached out from the blankets, it groped about the floor for the spectacles beneath the bunk. I picked them up. Then Sammy appeared with his other hand shielding his eyes. I passed him the spectacles and also a cigarette. When we inhaled he went into a coughing paroxysm. Jesus Christ, he managed to gasp.

Never mind, just think of the bacon and eggs, and these boiled tomatoes.

Chas had pulled his jeans out from underneath

his bunk and was dressing. He glanced at Sammy:
Some smells coming from your side last night.

Ah give us peace.

Chas is right, I said, fucking ridiculous. I'm complaining to Joe about it.

Ah shut up. Anyhow, when you get to my age it's
all you're bloody good for.

Chas grinned. A different story last night – you
and that auld wife of yours! I could hardly get to
sleep for thinking about it. Aye and I'll be telling
her what you said next time I see her.

Last time I let yous get me drunk, chuckled
Sammy. I'll no have a secret left by the time we get
back down the road... And he tugged the blankets
up over his shoulders. Me and Chas went into the
kitchenette for a wash. When we returned Sammy
was sitting up and knotting the laces on his boots,
ready to leave. Ach, he said, I cant be bothered
washing. I'll wait till we get to the canteen.

Clatty auld bastard, I said.

Not at all. It's to do with the natural oils son
– that's how yous pair keep getting hit by the
midges.

Rubbish, said Chas, you're a clatty auld cunt.

We parked in the place behind the canteen. Nobody
was around. It was a Saturday, but even so, the

three of us were always first into the canteen each morning. The woman smiled. As she dished out the grub she said, You lot were the worse for wear last night.

Aye, said Chas, what happened to that dance you promised us?

Dance! you couldnt walk never mind dance. You keelies, you're all the same.

Aw here wait a minute, cried Sammy. Less of that race-relations patter if you dont mind.

It's these teuchters Sammy, I said, they're all the same so they arc. Sooner we see a subway the better.

Away with your subways! The woman was piling the boiled tomatoes and bacon onto my plate... What're you wanting subways for?

Never mind what we're wanting subways for! Chas chuckled.

Aye hen, grinned Sammy, you can do a lot on a subway!

Is that so! well just dont be trying any of that tonight.

We carried our trays across to the table near the big windows. Sammy returned them to the rack once we had taken off our stuff. Actually, he said, I dont think I'll go to the club the night.

Thank Christ for that!

Naw son seriously.

But dont count on it, grinned Chas. He winked as he sliced a piece of bacon and dipped it into the egg yolk. He'll be there spoiling everything as per fucking usual.

Naw Chas honest. I'll have to take a look at the car. That bloody chinking sound's beginning to annoy me – besides which, we're spending too much on the bevy so we are. O Christ, he added, this food, it's bloody marvellous. I've never eaten like this in my puff.

While he spoke me and Chas were automatically covering our plates. Sammy seldom put in his teeth this early.

I've got to agree with you, said Chas, it's some grub right enough.

I snorted. I'll never know what yous pair got married for.

Sammy grinned. Will you listen to the boy!

After the second mug of tea we went back to the car to get the working-gear. Even when Sammy opened the boot the smell of it hit us; first thing in the morning was always bad. The boilersuits we had had to borrow from the factory stores, they were stiff and reeking of sweat; probably they had been left behind years ago by some squad of subcontractors.

Chas had slapped himself on the wrist suddenly and he turned up the palm of his hand to show us the remains of a midge. Look, he said, a bit of fucking dust. Aye Sammy, we definitely need a tin of cream or something.

I'll see Joe.

O good, I said.

Sammy glanced at me.

The chlorine tank we were working on stood at the very rear of the factory, not too far from the lochside. Its lining was being renewed. We had to strip away the old stuff to prepare the way. The tank was about 40 feet high and about 18 in diameter. On top was a small outlet through which the scaffolders had passed down their equipment; a narrow walkway separated it from a factory out-building. There was also a very small tunnel at the foot which us three had to use; it was quite a tight fit, especially for Sammy.

To allow us maximum daylight the scaffolders had erected the interior staging with minimum equipment. The platforms on which we worked were spaced about 8 feet apart. When we finished stripping a section of old lining we had to shift most of the planks and boards to the next, to make it safe to work on. But generated light was also necessary. In fact it would probably have suited us to have had the maximum scaffolding stuff rather than extra daylight. It was safe enough but we had to be careful; since the tank was circular the platforms couldnt cover the entire 18 feet. Chas had spotted a potential problem in connection with this. It was a bevel in one side. He had pointed it out to us yesterday evening.

While he went off to switch on the compressor I fiddled around with the air-hoses, giving Sammy a chance to sneak on ahead into the tunnel; somewhere inside was a place where he planked the chisels and other stuff. He was a bit neurotic about thieving and wouldnt even tell us where he kept it all.

It was a fair climb to the section we were on. One of the snags of the job was this continual climbing. The chisels kept on bouncing out the hammer nozzles and it seemed like it was my job to go and get them – and when they fell they always fell to the bottom of the tank. Once Chas arrived we adjusted the hammers onto the air-hoses and fixed on the chisels then one by one we triggered off. Half an hour later we stopped. Earlier in the week I got a spark in my right eye; while along at the First-aid I discovered we were not supposed to stay longer than 30 minutes without at least having a quarter of an hour break out in the open.

Sammy had gone off to make his morning report by telephone to the depot. Back at the lochside he explained how Joe had been unable to make it up yesterday. They had needed him for an urgent job. But he would definitely arrive some time today.

Is that all? I said, What I mean is did they no even apologise?

Aye, what would've happened if we were skint! said Chas.

Well we werent skint.

That's no the point but.

I know it's no the bloody point. Sammy sniffed, then he nudged the spectacles up on his nose a bit. The trouble with you son you're a Commie.

Naw I'm no – a good Protestant.

Sammy snorted. After a moment he said, I could always have seen that whatsisname, Williams, he would've subbed us a few quid.

Aye and that'd be us begging again!

He's right, said Chas. They must be sick of the sight of us in this fucking place. Fucking boilersuits and breathing-masks by Christ we're never done.

Aw stop your moaning.

Heh, you definitely no going to the club the night?

None of your business.

Chas grinned, Course he's going. Saturday night!

Dirty auld bastard, he couldnt survive without sniff-
ing a woman.

Ah well, said Sammy, nothing wrong with sniff-
ing. And I'll tell you something . . .

We know we know – when you get to your age
it's all your fucking good for.

Sammy laughed.

Joe turned up in the afternoon, during one of the
breaks out the tank. We were at the shore, skliffing
pebbles on the surface of the water. The last time
he came we were doing exactly the same thing. The
time before that we had been standing gabbing to
one of the storemen, and it was pointless trying to
explain about conning the fellow out of a couple of
new boilersuits. Joe never heard explanations. His eyes
would glaze over.

Heh Joe, I said, the First-aid people said we were
supposed to get a quarter of an hour break every half
hour, because of the fumes, the chlorine and that.

Is that right... Joe nodded. He was lighting a
cigarette, then chipping the match into the loch.

That's what they said.

Aye, it's kind of muggy... He gazed towards
the head of the loch where several small boats were
sailing north, the gannets flying behind and making
their calls. He sniffed and glanced at his wristwatch,

and glanced at Sammy. Fancy showing me your bevel? he said.

Aye Joe.

They walked up the slope. We waited a bit before following. Joe had gone off alone, and Sammy paused for us to catch up with him. He's away to see if whatsisname's arrived yet – he's supposed to be coming in to see the bevel... Pulling a rag from a pocket he wiped his brow and neck, and then wrapped it round his head like a sweatband. Must be hitting the 80's, he grunted. I'll tell you something, we're better off in the fucking tank.

What did he say about it? said Chas. Did he say anything?

Sammy looked at him.

The bevel I mean.

Aw aye. Naw, he'll have to have a look.

Heh, I said, Sammy! d'you notice the way he went *your* bevel; *your* bevel. As if you'd put the fucking thing there yourself.

Ach it's just his way... Sammy continued walking.

Another thing, I said, I bet you he asks that cunt Williams about the quarter of an hour breaks.

No danger, said Chas.

In fact it wouldnt surprise me if he knew about it in the first place – just forgot to fucking tell us.

As usual, muttered Chas.

For God sake! Sammy stopped and glared at us.

Well no wonder Sammy, sometimes he treats us as if we were the three fucking stooges.

The boy's right, said Chas. I notice he's no saying anything about the wages.

They'll be in his bloody car.

Aye and they'll stay there as long as possible, just in case we nick away for a pint or something.

Sammy's face reddened; he nudged the spectacles up on his nose. He turned and strode on to the tunnel. We watched him crawling inside.

Chas shrugged. We've upset him now.

Ach, no wonder. He's letting Joe take the piss out him.

He's no really.

Well how come he's still climbing scaffolding at his fucking age? he should be permanent down in the depot.

True. Chas sniffed, Come on – we better go and show the auld cunt we still love him.

He was pounding away with the hammer. He ignored us while we were preparing our stuff. Finally he switched off the power. About bloody time and all, he said, get cracking. I thought yous had went for a pint right enough!

How could we! it's your fucking round.

Sammy shook his head and turned back to the wall of the tank again, and triggered off. Chas winked at me. We worked on steadily. Then without having to ask I knew we were past the half hour. I saw Chas pause to demist the goggles he wore; he adjusted his breathing-mask and shrugged when I gestured at my wrist. We continued with the hammers.

About 5 minutes later the signal came from below; somebody was climbing the scaffolding. Both Joe and Williams. We stopped work. Sammy went off to show them the bevel and me and Chas had a smoke, sitting on the platform. We could hear snatches of their conversation. Williams said something about Monday being a Bank Holiday and Chas started laughing quietly. I fucking knew it, he whispered, we've knocked it right off.

What d'you mean?

He shook his head, then he whispered: You still fancy having a go at the Ben?

Fucking right I do, climbing it, aye. How?

Ssh.

Heh, heh yous two! Joe was calling. We got up and climbed to the next platform. He and Williams stood beside each other. A couple of yards away Sammy stared at the floor, puffing at a cigarette and scratching his head. Joe gestured us closer and

said, I think we've got it beat. Look... he pointed
at a couple of planks. Now Chas, if you and Sammy
stand at the bottom end of them the boy'll be able
to go out and do the lining.

What?

See look... Joe tugged Chas by the elbow who
then stepped aside while Joe placed the planks one
on the other; he pushed them like that out over the
gap being caused by the bevelled side of the tank.
See what I mean? he said. And he wiped his hands.

Eh . . .

Look Chas . . .

But before Joe could continue Williams had
stepped forward. The thing is, he said, the weight.
You and Sammy, together you must make about 3
or 4 of the boy. If you two stand on the bottom end
of the planks he'll be able to get out at the top. You'll
balance him no bother.

Chas didnt reply and I glanced at Sammy.

Save us a hell of a lot of bother too, added Joe.
What d'you think?

Eh . . .

Joe sniffed and turned: What about yourself
Sammy?

Ah, I'm no too sure Joe, being honest.

I think it'll work fine, said Williams. He's light –
you two'll balance him easy.

We could use three planks if you like, said Joe.

O naw. Sammy glanced at him: You couldnt use three planks. Naw Joe they'd just spread, it'd have to be two.

Aye... Joe nodded. He took out a packet of cigarettes and offered them round everybody. What d'you reckon? he said to Chas.

Eh... Chas sniffed. Then he shook his head slowly. I'm no sure Joe.

Worth a try but eh? Joe turned to me. Eh young yin? what d'you think? could you give it a go?

After a moment Williams said, Wait a minute, I've got a suggestion. What weight d'you think I am?

I shrugged.

Well I'm a good bit heavier than you though, agreed? Now look, if you and one of your mates take one end then I'll go out the other. Well say the three of you.

That's better, grinned Joe.

Williams tapped himself on the belly and chuckled, Dont remind me! No, seriously... He looked to Sammy and Chas. The three of you to balance me as opposed to you two balancing the boy, what d'you say?

At least to give it a try, said Joe.

It's no the same thing, I said.

Yes, said Williams, it's only a try though.

Aye but the hammer. Sammy said, It's the hammer Mr Williams – once it starts vibrating and the rest of it.

I know, fair enough.

It's different from just standing there, I said.

Joe cleared his throat.

Tell you what, said Williams, while I'm out I'll give it a blast with a hammer, will that do you?

I didnt reply.

Ah come on, said Joe.

But it's no the same thing.

We're no saying it's the same thing.

I just want to see how it works, shrugged Williams.

There was a moment's silence then Sammy came across the platform. No harm in seeing how it works, he said. Come on Chas... He also waved me forwards onto the planks. I hesitated but he nodded me on. He stood at the back, me in the middle, Chas to the front.

Right then Tom, said Joe to Williams, and he passed him a hammer with the chisel already fixed onto the nozzle. You ever worked one before?

Dont tell me – you pull the trigger! He took the hammer, checked it was securely attached to the air-hose then gave it a short burst. He manoeuvred his way along the planks, moving out on the top end, right over the gap at the bevel. Okay? he said.

Fine, called Sammy.

He put the chisel to the lining and triggered it off; the planks spread and we lost our footing, the hammer clattering and Williams yelled, but he managed to twist and get half onto the edge of the platform, clinging there with his mouth gaping open. Joe and Chas were already to him and clutching his arms, then me and Sammy were there and helping. When he got up onto the platform he sat for a long time, until his breathing approached something more normal. Nobody spoke during it all. His face was really grey. Joe had taken his cigarettes out and passed them round again. When he had given Williams a light he said, How you feeling Tom?

Williams nodded.

We continued smoking without speaking.

Eventually he glanced at Joe: Think I could do with a breath of fresh air.

Joe nodded. The four of us climbed down with him coming in between; he was still shaky but he managed it okay. When we came out of the tunnel he said, Jesus Christ... He smiled and shook his head at us. Joe went with him.

*   *   *

Down at the lochside Joe reappeared, and distributed the wages and subsistence money. While we checked the contents against the pay-slips he gazed towards the foot of the loch. The mountain peaks were distinct. Below the summit of the Ben a helicopter was hovering. Joe watched it for a time. Good place this, he said, a rare view.

Full of tourists but. Sammy shook his head. Can hardly get moving for Germans.

Joe nodded, he lit a cigarette. Pity about that fucking bevel, he said, we'll no manage to get the scaffolders out till Tuesday at the earliest – probably Wednesday... He glanced in the direction of Sammy.

Aye.

Puts us back.

Sammy nodded. Then he sniffed. Mind you Joe there's a fair bit of clearing up we can be getting on with – all that stuff we've stripped and that.

Aye... Joe inhaled on the cigarette. It's a nuisance but.

How's thingwi – that whatsisname, Williams?

Aw he's fine, fine. A bit shaky.

Sammy nodded, he nudged the spectacles on his nose.

Heh look at that! Joe had turned and he pointed out to where a motor launch and a water skier could be seen. Christ sake! he said. And he stood watching them for a long while. At last he glanced at his wristwatch. He turned and snorted.

Sammy looked at him.

So where is it the night? the social club?

Doubt it Joe – bloody car, it's acting up again.

Joe nodded.

What about yourself?

Aw! The time I get back down the road... He sniffed and glanced back at the loch, then he said, I suppose, I suppose... He glanced at his wristwatch. Okay Sammy, mind and phone in as soon as the scaffolders arrive.

Will do.

And eh – just do as much as you can, in the tank and that.

Aye well I mean that clearing Joe , .

Once he had gone the three of us continued sitting there, smoking, not talking for a while.

The Hitchhiker

IT WAS A TERRIBLE night. From where we were passing the loch lay hidden in the mist and drenching rain. We followed the bend leading round and down towards the village. Each of us held an empty cardboard box above his head. The barman had given them to us, but though they were saturated they were definitely better than nothing. We had been trudging in silence. When we arrived at the bridge over the burn Chas said, There's your hitchhiker.

I glanced up, saw her standing by the gate into one of the small cottages. She appeared to be hesitating. But she went on in, and chapped at the door. A light came on and a youngish woman answered, she shook her head, pointed along the road. The three of us had passed beyond the gate. About 30 yards on I turned to look back, in time to see her entering the path up to the door of another cottage. A man answered and shut the door immediately. The girl was standing there staring up at the window above the door; the porchlight was switched off. Two huge rucksacks strapped onto her back and about her shoulders and when she was walking from the cottage she seemed bent under their weight. Young lassie like that, muttered Sammy. She shouldnt be walking the streets on a night like this.

Aye, said Chas, but she doesnt look as if she's got anywhere to go. It's a while since we saw her.

I nodded. I thought she'd have had a lift by this time. Soaked as well, I said. Look at her.

She's no the only one that's soaked, replied Sammy. Come on, let's move.

Wait a minute, Christ sake.

The girl had noticed us watching her, she quickened her pace in the opposite direction. Sammy said: She's feart.

What?

He grinned at me, indicating the cardboard boxes. The three of us standing gaping at her! what d'you expect son? Sammy paused: If she was my lassie... Naw, she shouldnt be out on a night like this.

Not her fault she cant get a lift.

Single lassies shoudnt go hitching on their tod.

Sammy's right, grinned Chas. No with bastards like us going about.

Come on yous pair... Sammy was already walking away: Catch pneumonia hanging about in weather like this.

Just a minute, wait till we see what happens.

He paused, glowering at me and grunting unintelligibly. Meanwhile the girl was in chapping on the door of the next cottage. The person who answered gestured along the road in our direction; but once the door had closed she gazed at us in a defiant way and carried on in the opposite direction.

Dirty bastards, I shook my head, not letting her in.

Chas laughed: I'd let her in in a minute.

Away you ya manky swine ye, cried Sammy. His eyebrows rose when he added, Still – she's got a nice wee arse on her.

These specs of yours must have Xray lenses to see through that anorak she's wearing.

Sammy grinned: Once you reach my age son . . .

Bet you she's a foreigner, said Chas.

A certainty, I nodded.

The girl had just about disappeared into the mist. She crossed over the bridge and I could no longer distinguish her. And a moment later the older man was saying: Right then I'm off.

Chas agreed, Might as well.

The pair of them continued on. I strode after them. Heh Sammy, can the lassie stay the night with us?

Dont be daft son.

How no?

No room.

There is, just about.

Nonsense.

Christ sake Sammy how would you like to be kipping in a ditch on a night like this, eh? fuck sake, no joke man I'm telling you.

God love us son; sharing a caravan with the three of us! you kidding? Anyhow, the lassie herself'd never wear it.

I'll go and tell her it'll be okay but. I mean she can have my bunk, I'll kip on the floor.

Chas was grinning. Sammy shook his head, he muttered: Goodsafuckingmaritans, I dont know what it is with yous at all.

Ach come on.

Sammy grunted: What d'you say Chas?

Nothing to do with me, he grinned.

Good on you Chas, I said.

Ah! Sammy shook his head: The lassie'll never wear it.

We'll see.

I passed him the carry-out of beer I had been holding and ran back and across the bridge but when I saw her I slowed down. She had stopped to shrug the rucksacks up more firmly on her shoulders. A few paces on and she stopped again. I caught up to her and said, Hello, but she ignored me. She continued walking.

Hello.

She halted. To see me she twisted her body to the side, she was raging. Glaring at me.

Have you no place to stay? I said.

She hoisted the rucksacks up and turned away, going as fast as she could. I went after her. She was really angry. Before I got my mouth open she stopped and yelled: What.

Have you not got a place for the night?

Pardon... She glanced along the road as she said this but there was nobody else in sight. Never anybody in sight in this place, right out in the middle of the wilds it was.

Dont worry. It's okay. You need a place for the night. A house, a place out the rain · eh?

What?

A place to stay the night?

You know?

Hotel, there's a hotel.

Yes yes yes hotel, hotel. She shrugged: It is too much. She looked at me directly and said, Please – I go.

Listen a minute; you can come back to our place. I have place.

I . . . do not understand.

You can come to our place, it's okay, a caravan.
Better than hanging about here getting soaked.

She pointed at my chest: You stay?

Aye, yes, I stay. Caravan.

No! And off she trudged.

I went after her. Listen it's okay, no bother –
it's not just me. Two friends, the three of us, it's
not... I mean it's okay, it'll be alright, honest.

She turned on me, raging. What a face. She cried:
1 2 3... And tapped the numbers out on her fingers.
1 2 3, she cried. All man and me.

She tapped 1 finger to her temple and went on
her way without hesitation. At the lane which led
up to the more modern cottages used by the forestry
workers she paused for an instant, then continued
along it and out of sight.

Inside the caravan Chas had opened a can of lager
for me while I was finishing drying my hair. Both
he and Sammy were already under the blankets but
they were sitting up, sipping lager and smoking. The
rain battered the sides and the roof and the windows
of the caravan.

Chas was saying: Did you manage to get through
to her but?

Get through to her! Course I didnt get fucking

through to her – thought I was going to rape her or something.

Hell of a blow to your ego son, eh! Sammy grinned.

Fuck my ego. Tell you one thing, I'll never sleep the night.

Aye you will, said Chas. You get used to it.

You never get used to it. Never mind but, Sammy chuckled, you can have a chug when we're asleep... He laid the can of beer on the floor next to his bunk and wiped his lips with his wrist; he took another cigarette from his packet and lighted it from the dowp-end of the one he had been smoking. He was still chuckling as he said: Mind fine when I was down in Doncaster . . .

Fuck Doncaster.

Chas laughed. Never mind him Sammy – let's hear it.

Naw, better no. Sammy smiled, Wouldnt be fair to the boy.

When I had dried my feet I walked into the kitchenette to hang up the towel. The top section of the window was open. I closed it. If anything the rain seemed to be getting heavier. And back in the main area Chas said: She'll be swimming out there.

Thanks, I said.

Thanks! Sammy snorted, You'd think it was him swimming!

I drank a mouthful of lager, sat down at the foot of my bunk, and lifted the cigarette one of them had left for me. Chas tossed me the matches. A few moments passed before Sammy muttered: Aye, just a pity you never thought to tell her about next door.

I looked at him.

The sparks, he said, they're no here tonight. Had to go back down to Glasgow for some reason.

What?

I'm no sure, I think they needed a bit of cable or something.

Jesus Christ! How in the name of fuck could you no've told me already ya stupid auld... I was grabbing my socks and my boots.

Sammy had begun laughing. I forgot son honest, I forgot, I forgot, honest.

Chas was also laughing. The two of them, sitting spluttering over their lager. Fine pair of mates yous are, I told them. Eh! Fuck sake, never've signed on by Christ if I'd known about yous two bastarn comedians. Aye, no wonder they keep dumping yous out in the wilds to work.

Will you listen to this boy? Sammy was chortling.

And Chas yelling: Aye, and me about to lend him my duffel coat as well.

Keeping to the grass verge at the side of the track I walked quickly along from the small group of caravans. The centre of the track was bogging. It was always bogging. Even during the short heatwave of the previous week it was bogging. Plastered in animal shit. Cows and sheep and hens, even a couple of skinny goats, they all trooped down here from the fleariden farm a couple of fields away. By the time I got to the road my boots and the bottoms of my jeans were in a hell of a mess. I headed along to the village. Village by Christ – half a dozen cottages and a general store cum post office and the bastards called it a village. Not even a boozer. You had to trek another couple of miles further on to a hotel if you wanted a pint.

Over the bridge I went up the lane to the modern cottages. Although the mist had lifted a bit it was black night but it wasnt too bad, the occasional porchlight having been left on. Where the lane ended I turned back. If she was here she was either sheltering, or hiding.

Round the bend I continued in the direction of the hotel. The rain had definitely lessened, moonlight was glinting on the waters of the loch. I saw her standing at a wee wall next to the carpark entrance, she was with a very old man who was dressed in yellow oilskins, a small yap of a terrier darted about in the weeds at the side of the road. My approach had been noted. The girl finished muttering something to him, and he nodded. She made a movement of some kind, her face had tightened; she stared in the direction of the loch.

Well, I said. Has she not got a place yet?

What was that? The old man leaning to hear me.

I said has she not got a place yet, the lassie, she was looking for a place.

O aye aye, a place.

Aye, a place, has she got one yet?

He waited a moment before shaking his head, and while he half gazed away from me he was saying: I've been telling her try up at Mrs Taylor's house.

Were you?

Aye, aye I was telling her to try there. You know Mrs Taylor's I would think.

Naw, I dont, I dont at all.

Is that right... he had glanced at me. You dont know her house then, aye, aye. No, I dont think she'd have any rooms at this time of night. Mrs Taylor, he shook his head. A queer woman that.

The girl turned her head, she was gazing in

through the carpark entrance. But her gaze had included me in its manoeuvre. Look, I told the old man. I'm living on that wee caravan site along past the village. There's a spare one next to where I am. Tell her she'd be alright in there for the night.

He looked at me.

Look it's empty, an empty caravan, she'll be on her tod, nothing to worry about for Christ sake.

The old man paused then stepped the paces to begin chattering to her in her own language. Eventually she nodded, without speaking. She'll go, he said to me.

I told him to tell her I would carry her rucksacks if she wanted. But she shook her head. He shrugged, and the two of us watched her hitch them up onto her shoulders; then she spoke very seriously with him, he smiled and patted her arm. And she was off.

I nodded to him and followed.

She stared directly in front of her thick hiking boots. We passed over the bridge and on to the turnoff for the site. A rumble from the mountains across the loch was followed by a strike of lightning that brightened the length of the bogging track. A crack of thunder. Look, I said, I might as well get a hold of your rucksacks along here, it's hell of a muddy... I pointed to the rucksacks indicating I should carry them. I helped them from her. She swung them down and I put one over each of my shoulders. Setting off on the grass verge I then heard her coming splashing along in the middle of the bog, not bothering at all.

The light was out in our caravan. I showed her to the one next, and opened the door for her, standing back to let her enter but she waved me inside first. Dumping the rucksacks on the floor of the kitchenette we went into the main area, it was the same size as the one shared by the three of us. These caravans were only really meant for two people. A stale smell of socks and sweat about the place, but it was fine apart from this, fairly tidy; the sparks must have given it a going over before returning to Glasgow, and they had taken all their gear with them.

The girl had her arms folded and her shoulders hunched, as if she had recently shivered. She stood with her back to the built-in wardrobe. I nodded and said: I'll be back in a minute.

Chas was snoring. I could see the red glow from Sammy's cigarette. He always had trouble getting to sleep unless drunk; this evening we'd only had 4 or 5 pints each over a period of maybe 3 hours. He said: I heard yous.

Any tea bags?

My jacket pocket.

I also collected two cups and the tin of condensed milk from the cupboard in the kitchenette. It's still teeming down out there, I whispered.

Aye.

She's soaked through. I hesitated, Okay then Sammy – goodnight.

Goodnight son.

I chapped on the door before entering. She was now sitting on a bunk but still wore both her anorak and her hiking boots, her hands thrust deep inside the anorak pockets. When I had made the tea she held the cupful in both hands. No food, I said.

Pardon?

Food, I've no food.

Ah. Yes... She placed the tea on the floor, drew a rucksack to her, unzipped it and brought out a plastic container from which she handed me a sandwich. Then she closed the container without taking one for herself.

After a few sips of tea she said, Tea very good.

Aye, you cant beat it.

She looked at me.

The tea, I said, you cant beat it – very very good.

Yes.

She refused a cigarette and when I had my own smoking she asked: You work.

Aye, yes.

Not stay? She gestured at the window. The rain pounding at it.

Naw, not stay. I grinned: I stay in Glasgow.

Ah, she nodded, my friend is Glasgow.

Great place Glasgow. You like it?

Glasgow very good.

Great stuff, have another cup of tea immediately.

She looked at me.

Tea – more tea?

She shook her head. You ah... You... She continued in french and finished with a shrug: I cannot say this with english.

I shrugged as well and as soon as I had swallowed the last of the tea I rose to put the cups on the draining board at the sink. The girl said, You go now.

I smiled. I go now.

Yes.

In the morning, tomorrow morning I'll be here.

Yes.

I paused at the door.

She half smiled. Tired, tired tired tired.

I nodded and said, Goodnight.

★   ★   ★

Both of them were washed and ready to leave when I woke up next morning. When Sammy was out of earshot I asked Chas if he thought he would mind if I was a bit late in. Ask him and see, was the reply. Sammy scratched his head when I did, he said: Okay but dont be all morning. I pulled the blankets up to my chin but as soon as I heard the car engine revving I got out of the bunk and dressed. Brushed my teeth, shaved.

Outside it was dry, fresh, a clear morning in June. Across the loch puffy clouds round the Ben. In the hotel bar the previous night Sammy had forecast a return of the warm weather, and it looked like he was going to be right. There was no reply when I chapped the door. I chapped again and went inside. Clothes strewn about the place, as if she had unpacked every last item. And her smell was here now.

She was sleeping on her side, facing into the wall. I stepped back out and chapped the door loudly. Rustling sounds. I clicked the door open.

No!

It's me.

No!

I remained with my hand on the door knob.

Come!

Her hair rumpled, a pair of jeans and a Tshirt

she was wearing, eyes almost closed; she moved
about picking things up off the floor and folding
them away into the rucksacks; so much stuff lying
it seemed odds against the rucksacks being able to
take it all. I filled the kettle and shoved it on to boil
the water. She looked up: Tea?

Aye, yes, tea.

Your friends?

Work.

Ah.

She stopped clearing up, she yawned while sitting
down on the bunk with her back to the wall and
her legs drawn up, resting her elbows on her knees.
She gazed over her shoulder, out of the window,
murmuring to herself in french.

You sleep okay?

Yes, she replied.

She had the plastic container out, the sandwiches
ready, when I came back with the tea.

I said, It's a great morning outside, really great.
The morning, outside, the weather, really beautiful.

Ah, yes... She looked out of the window again
and spoke in french, she shrugged.

Tea good?

Very very good, she smiled. She passed me the
plastic container.

Fine sandwiches, I told her. What kind of stuff is this?

Pardon?

I parted the 2 slices of bread.

O. Sausage. You like?

It's good.

Yes. Suddenly she laughed, she laughed and held up the sandwich she was eating: In Glasgow piece – a piece. Yes?

Christ.

She laughed again, flicking the hair from her face: My friend in Glasgow she say peez, geez peez pleez.

That's right geeza piece, I grinned. Heh, more tea? fancy some more tea?

She nodded.

At the turnoff for the Mallaig Road we shook hands in a solemn sort of way, and she headed along in that direction, her gaze to where the boots were taking her. I watched until she reached the first bend on the road. She hadnt looked back at all.

When I banged out the signal the hammering halted and I crawled through the short narrow tunnel into the big chlorine tank we were relining. I climbed the scaffolding. The two of them were now sitting on

the edge of the platform, their legs dangling over,
having a smoke. Without speaking I got the working
gear on, pulled the safety-helmet, the goggles and
the breathing mask into their right positions about
my head. While tugging the sweatband down to my
brow a loud snort came from Sammy, and he said:
Looks like he's decided not to speak.

Aye, said Chas.

Waiting for us to ask I suppose.

Must be.

God love us.

A moment later Chas glanced at me: Well?

Well what?

Well?

Well well well.

Hh, Christ.

Ach never bother with him, grunted Sammy.

But Chas said: Did you or didnt you?

What? What d'you mean?

Did you or fucking didnt you?

Did I or didnt I what?

Sammy sighed: Aye or naw, that's all he's asking.

Is it? I laughed.

Orange bastard, muttered Sammy.

So you did then, Chas asked.

Did what?

Ah fuck off.

What's up.

What's up! Chas said, Are you going to tell us? aye or naw!

I had a look at the hammer to make sure it was properly adjusted onto the pressurised air-hose, then got myself a chisel. By the way, I said, thanks for bringing my gear up from below, makes a difference having good mates on a job like this.

Sammy gazed at me. He said to Chas: You wouldnt credit it – look at him, he's not going to tell us anything right enough. Tell you something for nothing Chas it's the last time the cunt'll even smell one of these tea bags of mine.

That goes for my duffel coat, grunted Chas.

I fixed the chisel into the nozzle of the hammer, and began whistling.

Fuck off, cried Chas.

Ach. Never bother, muttered Sammy, never bother. Who's interested anyhow!

I slung the hammer across my shoulder, tugging the airhose across to the place I had stopped at the day before. Both of them were watching me. I winked before pulling the goggles down over my eyes, triggered off the hammer.

Pictures

HE WASNT REALLY watching the picture he was just sitting there wondering on things; the world seemed so pathetic the way out was a straight destruction of it, but that was fucking daft, thinking like that; a better way out was the destruction of himself, the destruction of himself meant the destruction of the world anyway because with him not there his world wouldnt be either. That was better. He actually smiled at the thought; then glanced sideways to see if it had been noticed. But it didnt seem to have been. There was a female sitting along the row who was greeting. That was funny. He felt like asking her if there was a reason for it. A lot of females gret without reason. The maw was one. So was the sister, she gret all the time. She was the worst. Whenever you caught her unawares that was what would be happening, she would be roaring her eyes out. The idea of somebody roaring their eyes out, their eyes popping out their sockets because of the rush of water. Or maybe the water making them slippery inside the sockets so they slipped out, maybe that was what it was, if it was anything even remotely literal. No doubt it

would just prove to be a total figure of speech: eyes
did not go popping out of sockets. There was a sex
scene playing. The two actors playing a sex scene,
the female one raising the blanket to go down as
if maybe for oral intercourse, as if maybe she was
going to suck him. Maybe this is why the woman was
greeting along the row; maybe she once had this bad
experience where she was forced into doing that very
selfsame thing, years ago, when she was at a tender
age, or else just it was totally against her wishes
maybe. And she wouldnt want reminding of it. And
look what happens, in she comes to see a picture in
good faith and innocence, and straight away has to
meet up with that terrible ancient horror

or else she enjoyed her feelings of anguish and had
come along because of it, a kind of masochism or
something, having heard from one of her pals about
the sort of explicit – and maybe even exploitative –
sex scenes to expect if she did. That was the director
to blame anyway. In the pictures he was involved in
something like this usually happened, and there was
usually violence as well, like in this one murder. And
people would end up in bad emotional states. Was
it right that it should be like this? It was okay for
somebody like him – the director – but what about
other folk, ordinary folk, them without the security,
the overall security, the ones that actually went to

watch his fucking pictures! The thought was enough
to make you angry but it was best to just find it funny
if you could, if you could manage it. He nodded and
started grinning – it was best to. But it wasnt funny
at all in fact it was quite annoying, really fucking
annoying, and you could get angry about it, the way
these bastards in the film industry got away with it.

And there was that female now, her along the
row. He felt like shouting to her: What's up missis?
Something wrong?

God Almighty but, the poor woman, maybe there
was something bad up with her; he felt like finding
out, maybe he should ask, maybe it was some bastard
in a chair nearby, maybe wanking or something
because of the sex scene, and here was the woman
within perception distance – listening distance –
having to put up with it, and it maybe reminding her
of a terrible time when she was younger, just a lassie,
and was maybe forced into some sort of situation,
some kind of similar kind of thing. So fucking awful
the way lassies sometimes get treated.

But it had to come back to the director, he it was to
blame, it was this movie making the guy wank in the
first place, if he hadnt been showing the provocative
sexy scenes it wouldnt be fucking happening. There
was a lot to be said for censorship. If a censor had
seen this he would have censored it and then the

woman maybe wouldnt be greeting. But no, it was
more serious than that. Definitely. It was. She was
definitely greeting for a reason, a real reason, she had
to be – it was obvious; it had just been going on too
long. If it had stopped once the scene changed then
it would have been different, but it didnt. And the
woman actor was back up the bed and her and the
guy were kissing in the ordinary mouth-to-mouth
clinch so if the oral carry-on had been the problem
it was all over now and the woman should have
been drying her tears. So it was obviously serious
and had nothing to do with sex at all – the kind
that was up on the screen at least. Maybe he should
ask her, try to help. There were no attendants about.
That was typical of course for matinée programmes,
the management aye worked short-handed, cutting
down on overheads and all the rest of it. This meant
attendants were a rarity and the audience ran the
risk of getting bothered by idiots. Once upon a time
a lassie he knew was a cinema attendant. She used
to have to walk down the aisle selling ice-creams,
lollipops and popcorn at the interval; and they tried
to get her to wear a short mini-skirt and do wee
curtseys to the customers. But they obviously didnt
know this lassie who was a fucking warrior, a warrior.
She quite liked wearing short mini-skirts but only to
suit herself. If she wanted to wear them she would

wear them, but it was only for her own pleasure, she
would please herself. She used to get annoyed with
the management for other reasons as well; they used
to get her to wear this wee badge with her name on it
so it meant all the guys looked at it and knew what it
was and they shouted it out when they met her on the
street. Heh Susan! Susaaaaan! And then they would
all laugh and make jokes about her tits. It was really
bad. And bad as well if you were out with her if you
were a guy because it meant you wound up having
to get involved and that could mean a doing if you
were just one against a few. She was good too, until
she fucked off without telling him. He phoned her
up one night at tea-time and she wasnt in, it was her
flatmate. And her flatmate told him she had went
away, she had just went away. She had been talking
about it for a while but it was still unexpected when
it happened. Probably Manchester it was she went
to. He had had his chance. He could have went with
her. She hadnt asked him, but he could have if he
had wanted. It was his own fault he hadnt, his own
fault. She had gave him plenty of opportunities. So
it was his own fault. So he never heard of her again.
It was funny the way you lost track of folk, folk you
thought you would know for life; suddenly they just
werent there and you were on your ownsome. This
seemed to happen to him a lot. You met folk and got

on well with them but then over a period of time yous
drifted away from each other – the same as the guys
you knew at school, suddenly yous never even spoke
to each other. That was just that, finished, fucking
zero. It was funny. Sometimes it was enough to
make you greet. Maybe this is what was up with the
female along the row, she was just lonely, needing
somebody to talk to God he knew the feeling, that
was him as well – maybe he should just actually lean
across and talk to her. Could he do that? So incredible an idea. But it was known as communication,
you started talking to somebody, your neighbour.
Communication. You took a deep breath and the
rest of it, you fucking just leaned across and went
'Hullo there!' Except when it's a male saying it to
a female it becomes different. She had the hanky up
at the side of her eyes. She looked fucking awful. He
leaned over a bit and spoke to her:

Hullo there missis. Are you okay?

The woman glanced at him.

He smiled. He shrugged and whispered, You were
greeting and eh . . . you alright?

She nodded.

I couldnt get you something maybe, a coffee or a
tea or something, they've got them at the foyer . . .

She stared at him and he got a sudden terrible
dread she was going to start screaming it was fucking

excruciating it was excruciating you felt like stuffing
your fingers into your ears, he took a deep breath.

There wasnt anybody roundabout except an old
dear at the far end of the row. That was lucky.

Maybe there *was* something up with her right
enough. Or else maybe she was fucking mental –
mentally disturbed – and just didnt have anywhere
to go. Genuine. Poor woman. God. But folk were
getting chucked out on the street these days; healthy
or unhealthy, it didnt matter, the powers-that-be just
turfed you out and they didnt care where you landed,
the streets were full of cunts needing looked after,
folk that should have been in nursing homes getting
cared for. She was maybe one of them, just in here
out the cold for a couple of hours peace and quiet.
And then look at what she has to contend with up on
the bloody screen...! God sake! In for a couple of
hours peace and quiet and you wind up confronting
all sorts of terrible stuff in pictures like this one the
now. Maybe censors were the answer. Maybe they
would safeguard folk like this woman. But how?
How would they do it, the censors, how would they
manage it? No by sticking the cinemas full of Walt
Disney fucking fairyland. Who would go for a start?
No him anyway, he hated that kind of shite. Imagine
paying the entrance fee for that, fucking cartoons.
He leant across:

Ye sure you dont want a coffee?

She shut her eyes, shaking her head for a moment. She wasnt as old as he had thought either. She laid the hand holding the hanky on her lap and the other hand she kept at the side of her chin, her head now tilted at an angle. She kept looking at the screen.

I was going to get one for myself. So I could get one for you while I was at it . . .

She turned to face him then; and she said, Could you?

Aye, that's what I'm saying.

Thanks, you're a pal.

Milk and sugar?

Just milk.

He hesitated but managed to just get up, giving her a swift smile and not saying anything more, just edging his way along the row. He had to pass by the old dear sitting in the end seat and she gave him a look before holding her shopping bags in to her feet to let him past, and he nodded to her quite briskly. He walked up the aisle and down the steps, pushing his way out into the corridor. Thick carpets and dim lighting. He grinned suddenly, then began chuckling. How come he had nodded at the old dear like that? She was as old as his grannie! God Almighty! But it was to show her he was relaxed. That was how he had done it, that was how he had done it. If he hadnt been relaxed he would never have bloody managed it because it would have been beyond him.

Cinema 2 was showing a comedy. He had seen it a week ago. He wasnt that keen on comedies, they were usually boring. He continued past the corridor entrance. There was an empty ice-cream carton sitting on the floor in such a way you felt somebody had placed it there intentionally. Probably they had. He used to have the selfsame habit when he was a boy – thirteen or something – he used to do things to make them seem like accidental events. If he was smoking and finished with the fag he would stick it upright on the floor to make it look like somebody had just tossed it away and it had landed like that as a fluke.

He used to go about doing all sorts of stupid things. Yet when you looked at them; they werent all that fucking stupid.

What else did he used to do? He used to leave stuff like empty bottles standing on the tops of stones and boulders, but trying to make it look like they had just landed that way accidentally. To make folk imagine alien things were happening here on planet Earth and they were happening for a reason, a purpose.

He was a funny wee cunt when he was a boy. Looking back you had to admit it.

James Kelman

The woman at the kiosk passed him the change from the till; she was in the middle of chatting with the cashier and didnt watch him after she had put the money on the counter so he lifted a bar of chocolate, slid it up his jacket sleeve. One was plenty. He took the two wee containers of milk and the packet of lump sugar for himself.

It was raining outside. He could see folk walking past with the brollies up. And the streetlights were on. It would soon be tea-time.

He didnt take the chocolate bar from his sleeve until along the corridor and beyond the Cinemas 1 and 2, which were the most popular and had the biggest auditoriums – but there were usually cunts talking in them, that was the drawback, when you were trying to listen to the movie, they held fucking conversations. He had to lay the cartons of coffee down on the floor, then he stuck his hand in his side jacket pocket, letting the bar slide straight in from the sleeve. He was going to give it to her, the woman. He wasnt that bothered about chocolate himself. And anyway, in his experience females liked chocolate more than males. They had a sweet tooth.

That was one of these totally incredible expressions, a sweet tooth. What did it actually mean? He used to think it meant something like a soft tooth, that you had a tooth that was literally soft, made of something like soft putty. When he was a boy he had a sweet tooth. But probably all boys had sweet tooths. And all lassies as well. All weans the world over in fact, they all liked sweeties and chocolate, ice-cream and lollipops, popcorn.

She was sitting in a semi-motionless way when he got back to the seat and it was like she was asleep, her eyelids not flickering at all. Here's your coffee, he said, milk with no sugar, is that right?

Ta.

He sat down in his old seat after an eternity of decision-making to do with whether or not he could just sit down next to her, on the seat next to hers; but he couldnt, it would have been a bit out of order, as if just because he had bought her a fucking coffee it gave him the right of fucking trying to sit next to her and chat her up, as if he was trying to get off with her - which is what women were aye having to put up with. The best people to be women were men because of the way they were, the differences between them, their sexuality, because they could get sex any time they like just about whereas men were usually wanting it all the time but couldnt fucking get it - it was a joke, the way it worked like that, a joke of nature, them that wanted it no getting it and them that didnt want it having to get it all the time. The bar of chocolate. He took it out his pocket and glanced at it; an Aero peppermint; he passed it across, having to tap her elbow because she was staring up at the screen.

Here. It's a spare one. He shrugged, I'm no needing it. I'm no really a chocolate-lover anyway, to be honest, I've no got a sweet tooth, the proverbial sweet tooth. He shrugged again as he held it to her.

Oh I dont want that, she said out loud, her nose wrinkling as she frowned, holding her hand up to stop him. And he glanced sideways to see if folk had heard her and were maybe watching. He whispered: How no? It's alright.

Oh naw pal I just dont eat them – Aero peppermints – any kind of bar of chocolate in fact, being honest, I dont eat them.

Is it a diet like?

Aye. Thanks for the coffee but.

That's alright.

You're no offended?

Naw. I'll eat it myself. On second thoughts I'll no, I'll keep it for later. He stuck it back into his pocket and studied the screen while sipping the coffee which was far too milky it was like water. Funny, how they said something was coffee and then sold you a cup of fucking water with just a splash – a toty wee splash – of brown stuff, to kid you on. Total con. They did the selfsame thing with tea, they charged you for tea but served you with milk and water and another wee splash of brown, a different tasting one. You couldnt trust them. But it was hard to trust people anyway, even at the best of times. You were actually daft if you trusted them at all. At any time. How could you? You couldnt. Cause they aye turned round and fucked you in some way or another. That was his experience.

The film would soon be done, thank God. It was a murder picture, it was about a guy that was a mass-murderer, he kills all sorts of folk. A good-looking fellow too, handsome, then he goes bad and starts all the killing, women mainly, except for a couple of guys that get in his way, security men in the hostel, it was a nurses' hostel, full of women, and a lot of them fancy him, the guy, the murderer, he gets off with them first, screws them, then after he's screwed them he kills them – terrible. And no pity at all.

But sometimes you could feel like murdering somebody yourself in a way, because people were so fucking awful at times, you helped them out and nothing happened, they just turned round and didnt thank you, just took it like it was their due. His landlord was like that, the guy that owned the house he stayed in, he was a foreigner, sometimes you helped him out and he didnt even thank you, just looked at you like you were a piece of shite, like you were supposed to do it because you stayed in one of his fucking bedsits, as if it was part of your fucking rent or something.

He was sick of the coffee, he leaned to place the carton on the floor beneath the seat. He grimaced at the woman. She didnt notice, being engrossed in the picture. To look at her now you would hardly credit she had been greeting her eyes out quarter-of-an-hour ago. Incredible, the way some females greet, they turn it off and turn it on. He was going straight home, straight fucking home, to make the tea, that was what he was going to fucking do, right fucking now. Hamburger and potatoes and beans or something, chips. He was starving. He had been sitting here for two hours and it was fucking hopeless, you werent able to concentrate. You came to the pictures nowadays and you couldnt even get concentrating on the thing on the screen because

because it wasnt worth watching, that was the basic fact, because something in it usually went wrong, it turned out wrong, and so you wound up you just sat thinking about your life for fuck sake and then you started feeling like pressing the destruct button everything was so bad. No wonder she had been fucking greeting. It was probably just cause she was feeling so fucking awful depressed. About nothing in particular. You didnt have to feel depressed about something, no in particular, because there was so much of it.

The bar of chocolate in his pocket. Maybe he should just eat it himself for God's sake! He shook his head, grinning; sometimes he was a fucking numbskull. Imagine but, when he was a boy, leaving all these dowps lying vertical like that, just so somebody passing by would think they had landed that way! It was funny being a wean, you did these stupid things. And you never for one minute thought life would turn out the way it did. You never for example thought you would be sitting in the pictures waiting for the afternoon matinée to finish so you could go fucking home to make your tea, to a bedsitter as well. You would've thought for one thing that you'd have had a lassie to do it for you, a wife maybe, cause that's the way things are supposed to be. That was the way life was supposed to behave. When you were a boy anyway. You knew better once you got older. But what about lassies? Lassies were just so totally different. You just never fucking knew with them. You never knew what they thought, what they ever expected. They always expected things to happen and you never knew what it was, these things they expected, you were supposed to do.

What age was she? Older than him anyway, maybe thirty, thirty-five. Maybe even younger but it was hard to tell. She would've had a hard life. Definitely. Okay but everybody has a hard life. And she was on a diet. Most females are on a diet. She wasnt wearing a hat. Most females were these days, they were wearing hats, they seemed to be, even young lassies, they seemed to be as well; it was the fashion.

The more he thought about it the more he started thinking she might be on the game, a prostitute. He glanced at her out the side of his eye. It was definitely possible. She was good-looking and she was a bit hard, a bit tough, she was probably wearing a lot of make-up. Mostly all females wore make-up so you couldnt really count that. What else? Did she have on a ring? Aye, and quite a few, different ones, on her different fingers. She shall have music wherever she goes. Rings on her fingers and rings on her toes. Bells on her toes. She had black hair, or maybe it was just dark, it was hard to see properly because of the light; and her eyebrows went in a high curve. Maybe she *was* on the game and she had got a hard time from a punter, or else somebody was pimping for her and had gave her a doing, or else telt her he was going to give her one later, if she didnt do the business, if she didnt go out and make a few quid. Maybe her face was bruised. Maybe she had got a right kicking. And she wouldnt have been able to fight back, because she was a woman and wasnt strong

enough, she wasnt powerful enough, she would just
have to take it, to do it, what she was telt, to just do it.
God Almighty. It was like a form of living hell. Men
should go on the game to find out what like it was, a
form of living hell – that's what it was like. He should
know, when he was a boy he had once went with a
man for money and it was a horror, a horror story.
Except it was real. He had just needed the dough and
he knew about how to do it down the amusements,
and he had went and fucking done it and that was
that. But it was bad, a horror, a living hell. Getting
gripped by the wrist so hard you couldnt have got
away, but making it look like it was natural, like he
was your da maybe, marching you into the toilet, the
public toilet. Getting marched into the public toilet.
People seeing you as well, other guys, them seeing
you and you feeling like they knew, it was obvious,
him marching you like that, the way he was marching
you. Then the cubicle door shut and he was trapped,
you were trapped, that was that, you were trapped,
and it was so bad it was like a horror story except
it was real, a living hell, because he could have done
anything and you couldnt have stopped him because
he was a man and he was strong and you were just a
boy, nothing, to him you were just nothing. And you
couldnt shout or fucking do anything about it really
either because

because you were no just fucking feart you were in it
along with him, you were, you were in cahoots, you
were in cahoots with the guy, that was what it was,
the bad fucking bit, you were in cahoots with him,
it was like you had made a bargain, so that was that.
But him gripping you the way he was! What a grip!
So you had to just submit, what else could you do.
You had to just submit, you couldnt scream nor fuck
all. Nothing like that. Men coming into the urinals
for a pish, no knowing what was going on behind
the door and him breathing on you and feeling you
up, and grabbing you hard, no even soft, no even
caring if he had tore your clothes. What the wonder
was that nobody could hear either because of the
rustling noises the way he had you pressed against
the wall and then you having to do it to him, to
wank him, him forcing your hand and it was like
suffocating him forcing his chest against your face
and then coming over you, no even telling you or
moving so you could avoid it it was just no fair at
all, all over your shirt and trousers, it was terrible,
a horror story, because after he went away you had
to clean it all up and it wouldnt wipe off properly,
all the stains, the way it had sunk in and it was like
glue all glistening, having to go home on the subway
with it: broad daylight.

For a pile of loose change as well. How much was

it again? No even a pound, fifty stupid pence or something, ten bob. Probably no even that, probably it was something like forty pee, he just stuck it into his hand, some loose change. What did prostitutes get? what did they get? women, back then, nine year ago. It was probably about five quid if it was a short time; a tenner maybe if it was all night. That was enough to make anybody greet. But you could spend your life greeting, like his fucking sister. Because that was the thing about it, about life, it was pathetic, you felt like pressing the destruct button all the time, you kept seeing all these people, ones like the woman, the old dear at the end of the row, plus even himself as a boy, you had to even feel sorry for him, for himself, when he was a boy, you had to even feel sorry for yourself, yourfuckingself. What a fucking joke. A comedy. Life was a comedy for nearly everybody in the world. You could actually sympathise with that guy up on the screen. You could, you could sympathise with him. And he was a mass-murderer.

He glanced at the woman along the row and smiled at her, but then he frowned, he glared. You shouldnt be sympathising with a mass-murderer. You shouldnt. That was that fucking director's fault. That happened in his pictures, you started feeling sympathy for fucking murderers. How come it wasnt for the victims. They were the ones that needed it.

No the actual perpetrators. That was probably how she had been greeting, the woman, because of the fucking victims, she was a victim, and that's who it was happening to, the fucking victims. He wanted to go home, right now, he wanted out of it, right fucking out of it right fucking now it was a free country and he wanted to get away home for his fucking tea. He glanced along at her, to see what she was doing. She was still holding the carton of coffee, engrossed in the picture. The old dear as well. It was just him. He was the only one that couldnt concentrate. That was that nowadays, how he never seemed able to concentrate, it never fucking seemed to work any more, you couldnt blank it out. He kicked his coffee over. It was a mistake. But he was glad he had done it. He wished they had all fucking seen; it would sort them out, wondering how come he had done it, if it was meant; he got up off the chair and edged his way along to the end of the row, watching he didnt bump into her as he went; she never so much as glanced at him, then the old dear moving her bags in to let him pass, giving him a look as he went, fuck her, even if he stood on one of them with eggs in it, bastard, he just felt so fucking bad, so fucking bad.

Lassies Are Trained That Way

THE LASSIE CAME in on her own; she glanced roundabout then continued on past the *Ladies*, heading into the lounge. Minutes later she was back again, squinting this way and that, as if letting it be known she was only here because she was meeting somebody. When she arrived beside him at the bar there was a frown on her face. She asked the woman serving for a gin and orange-ade, stressing the orangeade, how she didnt want natural fruit juice or the diluting stuff. She was good-looking. She had on a pair of trousers and a wideish style of jersey. Eventually he spoke to her. He gave her a smile at the same time:

Has he gave you a dizzy?

The lassie ignored him.

Has he stood you up? he said, smiling. Then he drank a mouthful of lager. In some ways he hadnt been expecting any response, even though he was just being friendly, taking her at face value and trying to ease her feelings; get her to relax a bit. This wasnt the best of pubs for single women, being frank about it – not the worst, but definitely not the best.

Her eyes were smallish, brown, nice. He liked her looks. Okay. What is there to that? There can be strong feelings between the sexes. He was attracted to her. Fine. But even more than that: probably if something bad was happening he would have been first there, right at her elbow. It was a big brotherish feeling. He used to have a couple of wee sisters. Still has! Just that they are no longer wee. They are married women, with families of their own. He used to be a married man with a family of his own! Which simply means, to cut the crap, that him and his wife dont see eye-to-eye anymore. If they ever did. She doesnt live with him. And he doesnt live with her. They separated a year-and-a-half ago. He spent too much time boozing down the pub. Too much time out the house. That was the problem, he spent too much time out the house. The work did it. The kind of job he had is the kind that puts pressure on you. And what happens but you wind up in the pub drowning your sorrows.

The lassie with the brown eyes, she was standing beside him. He didnt know what she was maybe she was a student. Although she was older than the usual. But some of the older students came round here. Even during the day, when you might have expected them to be at their class getting their lessons, here they were, having a wee drink. He thought it livened

things up. Other folk didnt. Other folk didnt think
that at all. They thought it was better to have things
the opposite of livened up – deadened down – that's
what they thought it was better to have, that was their
preference. When they went into a pub they wanted
no people, no noise and no laughter, no music, no
life, no bloody fuck all, nothing, that's what they
liked, nothing, to walk into a pub and get faced
by nothing. How come they ever left their place of
abode? That was the real question. How come they
didnt just stay put, in their bloody house. Then they
would give other folk a break. If they were actually
interested in other folk then that's what they would
do, they would stay fucking indoors and give them a
bloody break. But they didnt do that. Out they came.
He couldnt be bothered with it, that kind of mental-
ity, he just couldnt be bothered with it. They were
misanthropes. The very last thing he ever wanted
to be. No matter how bad it got he would never
resort to that way of behaving. He genuinely thought
people should help one another. He did. He genuinely did. Something that was anathema nowadays
right enough, the way things were. But so what?
There's aye room for variety. Who wants everything
to be the same? Imagine it: a whole regiment of folk
all looking the same and then thinking the same
thoughts. That would be terrible, absolutely bloody

horrendous. You see some blokes going about, their faces tripping them. You wonder how come they ever set foot out the door, as if they just left the house to upset folk. A pain in the neck so they are. The kind that never does somebody a turn unless it's a bad yin. His wife's people were like that. They used to talk about him behind his back. They spoke about him to her, they carried tales. She believed them as well. Plus they did their chattering in front of the wee yins. Bad. If you've got to talk about somebody, okay, but no in front of the wee yins. Bringing somebody down like that. It's no right. There again but his wife didnt have to listen; nobody was forcing her, she could have ignored them, she could have told them to shut their bloody mouth.

The lassie was staring across the bar to beneath the gantry, to where all the bottles of beer were stacked, as if she was comparing all the different labels or something. Because she was feeling self-conscious. You could tell. And there was a mirror up above. She was maybe wanting to look into it to see if she could see somebody but she wasnt able to bring it off in case she wound up catching somebody else's eye. That was probably it. He gave her a smile but she ignored it. He didnt want to feel hurt because it would have been stupid. Not only stupid but ridiculous. She hadnt ignored him at all. She had just no seen him.

But she was no seeing anybody. Which is what lassies have to do in pubs. It's part of how they've got to act. He had a daughter himself and that's exactly what he would be telling her next time he saw her. You just cannot afford to take chances, no nowadays – different to when he was young. Aye, he said, young yins nowadays, they have it that wee bit harder.

And he glanced at her but she kept her stare fixed on the bottles beneath the gantry. Which was okay really because he had said it in such a way she would be able to do exactly that, ignore him, without feeling like she was giving him an insult at the same time. That kind of point was important between the sexes, between men and women, if ever they were to manage things together. He gave her another smile and she responded. She did. Her head looked up and she nodded. That was the irony. If you're looking for irony that's it. Plus as well the way things operate in conversation it was really up to her to make the next move, whatever it was, it was up to her.

The woman serving behind the bar was watching him. She was rinsing the glasses out at the sink. Her head was bent over as if she was attending totally to the job in hand but she wasnt, it was obvious. Probably because she knew he was married, thinking to herself: So he's like that is he; chatting up the young lassies, I might've bloody guessed, they're all the bloody same!

And that would make you laugh because he wasnt like that at all. No even just now when he was separated, when he was away living on his own. It was a total guess on her part and she was wrong. But women like to guess about men. They get their theories. And then they get surprised when the theories dont work out. She had seen him talk to the lassie and she just assumed he was trying to chat her up. It can be bad the way folk jump in and make their assumptions about you. And apart from his age what made her so sure he was married anyway? He had gave up wearing the band of gold a while ago and she was new in the job, still feeling her way; she was still finding out about folk and as far as he was concerned what could she know? almost nothing, it was just guesswork.

The woman was wearing a ring herself but that didnt even mean *she* was married. As far as a lot of females are concerned a band of gold's a handy thing to have pure and simple for the way it can ward off unwelcome attention. There again but let's be honest, most men dont even see a ring, and even if they do, so what? they just bloody ignore it.

The woman stopped rinsing glasses now to serve an auld bloke at the far end of the bar. He said something to her and she said something back and the two of them smiled. She had a quiet style with the customers, but she could crack funny wee jokes as well, the kind you never seem to hear at first – no till after the person that's told you has went away and you're left standing there and suddenly you think: Aye, right enough... This is the way it was with her. And then when you looked for her once it had dawned on you she was off and pouring the next guy's pint, she had forgot all about it. It was actually quite annoying. Although at the same time you've got to appreciate about women working in a pub, how they've got to develop an exterior else they'll no be able to cope. This one for example had a distracted appearance like she was always away thinking about bloody gas bills or something. Mind you that's probably what she was thinking about. Everything's so damn dear nowadays. He said it to the lassie. He frowned at her and added: Still and all, it wasnt that much better afore they got in, the tories.

She looked at him quite surprised. It was maybe the first time she had genuinely acknowledged he was a person. And it made him think it confirmed she was a student, but at the same time about her politics, that she was good and left-wing. He jerked his head in the direction of the woman serving behind the bar.

Her there, he said, I think she's a single parent; she looks like she goes about worried out of her skull because of the bills coming in – she'll have a tough time of it.

The lassie raised her eyebrows just; and that was that, she dropped her gaze. In fact she looked like she was tired, she did look like she was tired. But it was a certain kind of tiredness. The kind you dont like to see in young people – lassies maybe in particular, though maybe no.

I'm forty going on fifty, he said and he smiled, forty going on fifty. Naw but what I mean is I feel like I'm fifty instead of forty. No kidding. In fact I felt like I was fifty when I was thirty! It was one of the major bones of contention between me and the wife. She used to accuse me about it, being middle-aged. She used to say I was an auld man afore my time. No very nice eh? Accusing your husband of that.

He smiled as he shook his head, swigged a mouthful of beer. Mate of mine, he said, when I turned forty, at my birthday, I was asking him what like it was, turning it I mean, forty, and what he told me was it took him till he was past fifty to bloody get over it!

He smiled again, took his fags out for another smoke although he was trying to cut down. The lassie already was smoking. He lit one for himself.

I noticed you come in, he said, the way you walked ben the lounge and then came back here, like you were looking for somebody. I'm no being nosy, it's just an observation, I thought you were looking for somebody.

She had two brown moles on her cheek, just down from her right eye. They were funny, pretty and beautiful. It made him smile.

That was how I spoke to you, he went on, because I thought you were in looking for somebody and they hadnt showed up. I'm no meaning to be nosy, it was just I thought the way you looked, when you came in... He finished by giving a nod then inhaled deeply on his cigarette. He was beginning to blab and it was making her uncomfortable. He wasnt saying it right, what he was meaning to say, he was coming out with it wrong, as if it was a line he was giving her, a bit of patter.

She was just no wanting to talk. That was it. You could tell it a mile away. Then at the same time she wasnt wanting to be bloody rude. It was like she maybe didnt quite know how to handle the situation, as if she was under pressure. Maybe she would have handled things better if it had been a normal day, but for some reason the day wasnt normal. Maybe something bad had happened earlier on, at one of her classes, and she was still feeling the effects, the emotional upset. He wanted to tell her no to worry. She wasnt at her classes now.

Unless she thought he was acting too forward or something because he was talking to her – though as far as pubs go surely no, it was just what comes under the heading of being sociable. And we have to live with one another. Come on, if we arent even allowed to talk! Nowadays right enough you cant even take that for granted; it's as if you're supposed to go about kicking everybody in the teeth; you're no supposed to be friendly, if you're friendly they go and tell the polis and you wind up getting huckled for indecent assault. There again but folk have *had* to get that wee bit tougher nowadays, just to survive. He said to the lassie: Do you know what the trouble is? I'm talking about how things have got harder and tougher these past couple of years.

She kept her head lowered. It made him smile. He glanced over the counter but the woman was off serving other folk. He smiled again: You obviously dont want to know what the trouble is! And that's your privilege, that's your right. But I'm going to tell you anyhow!

Naw but seriously, he said, the way things are – society I'm meaning – it's just like auld Joxer says in that play by Sean O'Casey, the world's in a state of chassis. I'm talking about how capitalism and the

right-wing has got it all cornered, so selfishness is
running amok, everywhere you look, it's rampant –
no just here in Scotland but right across the whole of
the western world. It's bloody disgusting. Everybody
clawing at one another. Nobody gives a shit. We
just dont care anymore about what the neighbour
next door might be suffering. It's true. They can be
suffering. That auld woman up the stair for example,
take her, you've no seen her for how long? a week? a
fortnight? a bloody month? So what do you do do you
go up and keek through the letterbox? naw, do you
hell; nothing as simple that, what you do is go and
phone the bloody polis and get them to come and do
it for you. That's the way it is. So you come to rely on
people like the polis as if they were angels of mercy –
instead of what they are, the forces of law and order
for the rich and the wealthy, the upper class.

The lassie frowned.

Sorry, he said, am I talking too loud? I know
you're no supposed to nowadays. When you talk
about something you're really interested in you're
supposed to bloody keep it down, the noise level I
mean. So so much for your interest, if it happens to
be bloody genuine... He shook his head, sighing;
he drank from his pint of lager, glancing at her over
the rim of the glass, but she was managing not to look
at him. Funny how that happened. He could never

have managed it himself, to not speak to somebody who was speaking to you. He would have found it extremely difficult, to achieve, he would have found it really difficult. Maybe some folk were mentally equipped to carry that kind of thing off but he wasnt, he just didnt happen to be one of them – not that he would have wanted to be anyhow. Mind you, if he had been a lassie... But lassies are trained for it, in a manner of speaking; it's part of the growing-up process for them, young females. It doesnt happen with boys, just if you're a lassie, you've got to learn how not to talk; plus how not to look, you get trained how not to look. How not to look and how not to talk. You get trained how not to do things.

My mother was a talker, he said, God rest her she was a good auld stick. I liked my father but I have to admit it I loved my mother. She used to sing too. She's been dead for fifteen years. Fifteen years. A long time without your maw eh? I was just turned twenty-five when it happened. A long time ago.

The lassie smiled.

You're smiling, he said, but it's true. He tapped ash onto the floor and scraped the heel of his shoe over it, then inhaled deeply. He had loved his mother. It was funny to think that, but he had. And he missed her. Here he was a grown man, forty years of age, and he still missed his mammy. So what but? People do die. It's the way things are. Nobody can change it. The march of progress.

I dont believe in after-lives, he said, and I dont bloody believe in before-lives. Being honest about it I dont believe in any of your bloody through-the-looking-glass-lives at all. And that includes whatever you call it, Buddhism or Mohammedism or whatever the hell. There's the here and there's the now. Mind you, I'm no saying there's no a God, I'm just no saying there is one. What I will bloody say is I'm no very interested, one way or the other. What about yourself?

O... She smiled for a moment then she frowned almost immediately; she dragged on her cigarette and let the smoke out in a cloud. Then she dragged on it again but this time inhaled.

He shrugged. It's alright if you're not wanting to speak, I know how things are. Dont worry about it. Anyway, I'm doing enough chattering for the two of us! One thing but I will say – correct me if I'm wrong – your politics, they're like my own, we're both to the left. Eh?

She nodded very slightly, giving a very quick smile. Probably she was a wee bit suspicious. And if she wasnt she should've been; especially nowadays. Because you just never know who you're talking to. He gazed at her. There was something the . . .

And then he felt like giving her a kiss. It was so sudden and what an urge he had to turn away.

And he felt so sorry for her. He really did. He felt so sorry for her. How come he felt so sorry for her? It was almost like he was going to burst out greeting! How come? How come it was happening? He gulped a couple of times and took a puff on the fag, then another one. God. He bit on his lower lip; he stared across the bar to where a conversation was on the go between some guys he knew – just from drinking in here but, he didnt know them from outside – and didnt really want to either. Nothing amazing, he just found it difficult being in their company, it was a bit boring, if he had to be honest, nothing against them, the guys themselves. What was up? What was wrong? He blinked, he kept his eyelids shut for several moments.

A tiny wee amount of gin and orangeade was left in her glass. She was obviously trying to make it last for as long as possible. And she wouldnt allow him to buy her another. That was for definite. It was a thing about females. She was looking at the clock. That was another thing about them! Women! God! Strange people! He grinned at the lassie: Yous women! Yous're so different from us! Yous really are! Yous're so different!

She gazed at him.

Yous are but honest.

In what way?

O Christ in every way.

She nodded.

I mind when my daughter started her period if you dont mind me saying – I felt dead sorry for her. No kidding. Know how? Because she wasnt going to be a boy! He shook his head, smiling.

That's awful.

Naw, he said, what I mean . . .

But she had looked away from him in such a style that he stopped what it was he was going to say. Along the counter the woman serving was setting pints up for a group of young blokes who had just come in. He said, I dont mean it the way it sounds. The exact same thing happens with a pet, a wee kitten or a wee puppy, when it's newborn and it's just like any baby . . .

I dont want to hear this.

Naw but . . .

She shook her head. I dont want to hear it.

Aye but you dont know what I'm going to say.

I dont want to hear it. She smiled, then set her face straight, stubbed her fag out in the ashtray.

He had just been wanting to tell her how the things he liked as a boy he had wanted his wee lassie to get involved in, because he knew she would enjoy

them, that's all; nothing else, things like football and
climbing trees, jumping the burn; nothing special,
the usual, the usual crap, just the things boys did.
Of course she would go on and do the things lassies
did and she would enjoy them. He knew that. That
was what happened. And it was fine. But it wasnt the
point. It was something else, to do with a feeling, an
emotional thing. Surely you had to be allowed that?

He indicated her near-empty glass. D'you want
a drink?

No thanks.

He smiled.

I'm going in a minute.

He smiled again. There's barriers between us, the
sexes. But what you cannot deny is that we're drawn
to one another. We are: we're drawn to one another.
There's bonds of affection. And solidarity as well,
you get solidarity between us – definitely... That's
what I think anyhow – course I'm aulder than you...
When you get to my age you seem to see things that
wee bit clearer.

She looked at him. That's just nonsense.

I'm no saying you see everything clearer, just some
things.

She sighed.

I was reading in a book there about it – it was a
woman writer – she was saying how there's a type of

solace you can only receive from the opposite sex, a man from a woman a woman from a man.

It's nonsense.

It's no nonsense at all.

She paused for a moment, then replied, Yes it is. She looked away from him, off in the direction of the group of young blokes, one of whom stared at her. So blatant too, the way he did it. He just turned and stared at her, then he turned back to his pals. And the lassie shifted the way she was standing. She looked up at the clock and checked the time against her wristwatch.

They keep it quarter of an hour fast, he said. Common practice. A few of the customers complain right enough. But it's so they can get the doors shut on the button else the polis'll come in and do them for being late and they might lose their licence. So they say anyway. Mind you it's bloody annoying if you've come in looking to enjoy a last pint and then they start shouting at you and start grabbing the glass out your bloody hand. My auld da used to say it was the only business he knew where they threw out their best customers!

She didnt respond.

He grinned. I mean it's no as if they open quarter of an hour early in the morning! Look eh . . . are you sure I cant buy you one afore you go?

No, thanks.

He nodded.

I'm just leaving.

He never turned up then eh!

No.

Was it your boyfriend?

She shook her head.

D'you mind me asking you something. Are you a student?

Why d'you want to know?

I was just wondering.

Why?

Aw nothing.

She continued looking at him. He felt like he had been given a telling off. For about the third bloody time since she had come in. He swallowed the last of his lager and glanced sideways to see where the bar staff had got to. And then he said, Do you think it's possible for men and women to talk in a pub without it being misconstrued?

She paused. I think people should be able to stand at a bar without being pestered.

O you think you're being pestered? Sorry, I actually thought I was making conversation. That's how come I was talking to you, it's what's commonly known as being sociable. I didnt know I was pestering you.

She nodded.

Sorry.

It's just that I think people should be able to stand at the bar if that's what they want to do.

So do I, he said, so do I. That's what I think. I mean that's what I think. My own daughter's coming up for seventeen you know so I'm no exactly ignorant of the situation.

The woman behind the counter had reappeared and was looking along in his direction, like she had heard the word 'pester' and was just watching to see. He shook his head. It was like things were getting out of hand; you wanted to shout: Wait a minute! He frowned, then smiled. When he was a wee boy him and his brother and sisters would be right in the middle of a spot of mischief when suddenly the door would burst open and mammy would be standing there gripping the handle and glowering at them. And they would all be on the confessional stool immediately! She didnt have to fucking do anything! They'd all just start greeting and then cliping on one another! What a technique she had! It was superb! All she had to do was stand there! Everybody crumbled.

He grinned, shaking his head, and he called for a pint of lager. For a split second the woman didnt seem to hear him. Then she walked to the tap, started pouring the pint, staring at the lever very deliberately, as if she was making some sort of point. It was funny. Maybe she was a bit put out about something. Well that was her problem. If you've got to start safeguarding the feelings of everybody you meet on the planet then you'll have a hard time staying sane.

The lassie wasnt there.

Aye she was but she was across at the group of young guys. They looked like students as well. He didnt have anything against students. Although the danger was aye the same for kids from a working-class background, that it turned you against your own people. How many of them were forever going away to uni and then turning round and selling themselves to the highest bidder as soon as they'd got their certificates. Then usually they wound up abroad, if no England then the States or Canada or Australia, or Africa or New Zealand, it was all the same. Then they spent the rest of their lives keeping other folk down.

One of the young blokes laughed. It would have been easy to take it personally but that would have been stupid. Getting paranoiac is the simplest thing in the world. A gin and orangeade was on the counter in front of the lassie but she was paying for it out of her own purse. A young guy glanced across. Another one said something. But there was no point seeing it directed at yourself. The woman behind the bar was away serving another customer. The change back from the money for the pint of lager was lying on the counter. He put his hand out to get it.

Old Francis

HE WIPED THE bench dry enough to sit down, thrust his hands into his jacket pockets and hunched his shoulders, his chin coming down onto his chest. It was cold now and it hadnt been earlier, unless he just wasnt feeling it earlier. And he started shivering immediately, as if the thought had induced it. This was the worst yet. No question about it. If care wasnt taken things would degenerate even further. If that was possible. But of course it was possible. Anything was possible. Everything was possible. Every last thing in the world. A man in a training suit was approaching at a jog, a fastish sort of jog. The noise of his breathing, audible from a long way off. Frank stared at him, not caring in the slightest when it became obvious the jogger had noticed and was now a wee bit self-conscious in his run, as if his elbows were rotating in an unnatural manner. It was something to smile about. Joggers were always supposed to be so self-absorbed but here it seemed like they were just the same as the rut, the common rut, of whom Francis was definitely one. But then as he passed by the bench the jogger muttered something which ended in an 'sk' sound, perhaps 'brisk'. Could he have said something like 'brisk'? Brisk this morning. That was a fair probability, in reference to the weather. Autumn. The path by the side of the burn was deep in slimy leaves, decaying leaves, approaching that physical state where they were set to be reclaimed by the earth, unless perhaps along came the midgie men and they shovelled it all up and dumped it into the midgie motor then on to the rubbish dump where they would sprinkle aboard paraffin and so on and so forth till the day of judgement. And where was the jogger! Vanished. Without breaking stride he must have carried straight on and up the slow winding incline towards the bridge, where to vanish was the only outcome, leaving Francis alone with his thoughts.

These thoughts of Francis's were diabolical.

The sound of laughter. Laughter! Muffled, yes, but still, laughter. Could this be the case!! Truly? Or was it a form of eternal high jinks!!

Hearty stuff as well. Three blokes coming along the path from the same direction the jogger had appeared from. They noticed Francis. O yes, they soon spotted him. They couldnt miss him. It was not possible. If they had wanted to miss him they couldnt have. And they were taking stock of him and how the situation was in toto. They were going to get

money off of him, off of. One of them had strolled
on a little bit ahead; he was wearing a coat that must
have belonged to somebody else altogether, it was
really outlandish. Francis shook his head. The bloke
halted at the bench and looked at him:

You got twenty pence there jim, for the busfare
home?

Francis was frowning at the bloke's outfit. Sorry,
he said, but that's some coat you're wearing!

What?

Francis smiled.

Funny man.

Sorry, I'm no being sarcastic.

A funny man! he called to his two companions.
He's cracking funnies about my coat!

Surely no! said this one who was holding a bottle
by its neck.

Aye.

That's cheeky! He swigged from the bottle and
handed it on to the third man. Then he added:
Maybe he likes its style!

The first bloke nodded, he smiled briefly.

And he wants to buy it! Heh, maybe he wants to
buy it! Eh, d'you want to buy it?

Frank coughed and cleared his throat, and he
stared at the grass by his shoes, sparish clumps
of it amid the muddiness, many feets have stood

and so on. He raised his head and gazed at the second man; he was dangerous as well, every bit as dangerous. He noticed his pulse slowing now. Definitely, slowing. Therefore it must have been galloping. That's what Francis's pulse does, it gallops. Other cunts's pulses they just fucking stroll along at a safe distance from one's death's possibility. What was he on about now! Old Francis here! His death's possibility! Death: and/or its possibility. Was he about to get a stroke? Perhaps. He shook his head and smiled, then glanced at the first bloke who was gazing at him, and said: I didnt mean you to take it badly.

What?

Your coat. Frank shrugged, his hands still in his pockets. My comment... he shrugged again.

Your comment?

Aye, I didn't mean you to take it badly.

I never took it badly.

Frank nodded.

The second bloke laughed suddenly. Heh by the way, he said, when you come to think about it, the guy's right, your fucking coat, eh! Fucking comic cuts! Look at it!

And then he turned and sat down heavily, right next to him on the bench; and he stared straight into his eyes. Somebody whose body was saturated with alcohol. He was literally smelling. Literally actually smelling. Just like Francis right enough, he was smelling as well. Birds of a feather flock together. And what do they do when they are together? A word for booze ending in 'er'. Frank smiled, shaking his head. I'm skint, he said, I'm out the game. No point looking for dough off of me.

Off of. There it had come out again. It was peculiar the way such things happened.

The two blokes were watching him. So was the third. This third was holding the bottle now. And a sorry sight he was too, this third fellow, a poor looking cratur. His trousers were somebody else's; and that was for fucking definite. My my my. Frank shook his head and he called: Eh look, I'm no being sarcastic but that pair of trousers you're wearing I mean for God sake surely you could do a wee bit better, eh?

He glanced at the other two: Eh? surely yous could do a wee bit better than that?

What you talking about? asked the first bloke.

Your mate's trousers, they're fucking falling to bits. I mean look at his arse, his arse is fucking poking out!

And so it was, you could see part of the man's shirt tail poking out! Frank shook his head, but didnt smile. He gestured at the trousers.

He is a funny man right enough! said the second bloke.

Instead of answering him the first bloke just watched Frank, not showing much emotion at all, just in a very sort of cold manner, passionless. If he had been unsure of his ground at any time he was definitely not unsure now. It was him that was dangerous. Of the trio, it was him. Best just to humour him. Frank muttered, I'm skint. He shrugged and gazed over the path towards the burn.

You're skint.

Frank continued gazing over the path.

It's just a couple of bob we're looking for.

Sorry, I really am skint but.

The second bloke leaned closer and said: Snout?

Frank shook his head.

You've got no snout! The bloke didnt believe him. He just didnt believe him. He turned and gave an exaggerated look to his mates. It was as if he was just not able to believe it possible. Frank was taken aback. It was actually irritating. It really was. He was frowning at the fellow, then quickly he checked what the other one was doing. You never know, he might have been sneaking up behind him at the back of the bloody bench! It was downright fucking nonsensical. And yet it was the sort of incident you could credit. You were sitting down in an attempt to recover

a certain inner equilibrium when suddenly there
appear certain forces, seemingly arbitrary forces,
as if they had been called up by a positive evil.
Perhaps Augustine was right after all? Before he left
the Manicheans.

Twenty pence just, said the first.

Frank shook his head. He glanced at the bloke.
Look, I'm telling you the truth, I'm skint.

You've got a watch.

What – you kidding! Frank stared at him for a
moment; then he sniffed and cleared his throat,
gazed back over the path.

He has got a watch, said the second bloke.

And now the third stepped across to the bench,
and he handed the bottle to the first. Frank had
his hands out of his pockets and placed them onto
his kneecaps, gripping them, his knuckles showing white.

Did you miss your bus? asked the first.

Did you miss your bus! laughed the second.

And the third bloke just stared. Frank stared back
at him. Was he the leader after all? Perhaps he was
the one he would have to go for first, boot him
in the balls and then face the other pair. Fucking
bastards. Because if they thought he was going to
give them the watch just like that then they had
another think coming. Bastards. One thing he was

never was a coward. Bastards, he was never fucking a coward. He flexed his fingers then closed them over his kneecaps again, and he sighed, his shoulders drooping a bit. He stared over the path. It was as if they were aspects of the same person. That was what really was the dangerous thing.

The second bloke was speaking; he was saying, I dont think he even goes on public transport, this yin, I think he's a car-owner.

A car-owner! Frank grinned. I'm actually a train-owner! A train-owner! That was really funny. One of his better witticisms. A train-owner. Ha ha. Frank smiled. He would have to watch himself though, such comments, so unfunny as to approach the borderline.

What borderline? One of irrationality perhaps. A nonsensicality. A plain whimsy. Whimsy. There was a bird whistling in a tree nearby. D d d dooie. D d d dooie. Wee fucking bird, its own wee fucking heart and soul. D d d dooie. What was it looking for? It was looking for a mate. A wee female. A wee chookie. Aw the sin. My my my. My my my. And yet it was quite upsetting. It brought tears to the eye. If Frank could just heave a brick at the tree so it would get to fuck away out of this, this vale of misery. God. I need a drink, said Frank to the first bloke. He gestured at the bottle: D'you mind?

The man handed him the bottle.

The second looked at him, biding his time, waiting to see the outcome.

And the third bloke put his hands into his trouser pockets and strolled across the path, down to the small fence at the burn, where he leant his elbows.

The noise of the water, the current not being too strong, a gush more than anything, a continuous gushing sound, and quite reassuring. This freshness as well, it was good. The whole scene in fact, was very peaceful, very very peaceful; a deep tranquillity. Not yet 10 o'clock in the morning but so incredibly calm.

There was no label on the bottle. Francis frowned at this. What happened to the label? he said.

It fell off.

Is it hair lacquer or something?

Hair lacquer! laughed the second bloke.

It looks like it to me, replied Francis.

You dont have to fucking drink it you know!

Francis nodded; he studied the bottle. The liquid looked fine – as much as it was possible to tell from looking; but what was there could be told about a drink by looking at the outside of its bottle? He couldnt even tell what colour it was, although the actual glass was dark brownish. He raised the neck of the bottle, tilted his head and tasted a mouthful:

Christ it was fiery stuff! He shook his head at the two blokes, he seemed to be frowning but he wasnt. WWhhh! Fucking hot stuff this! he said.

Aye.

Francis had another go. Really fiery but warming, a good drink. He wiped his mouth and returned the bottle. Ta, he said.

I told you it was the mccoy, said the second bloke.

Did you?

Aye.

Mm. It's fucking hot, I'll say that!

Know what we call it?

Naw.

Sherry vindaloo!

Francis smiled. That was a good yin, sherry vindaloo. He'd remember it.

The first bloke nodded and repeated it: Sherry vindaloo.

The second bloke laughed and swigged some, he walked to hand it to the third who did a slightly peculiar thing, it was a full examination; he studied the bottle all round before taking a sip which must have finished it because the next thing he was leaning over the fence and dropping the bottle into the burn. Francis glanced at the first bloke but didnt say anything. Then he shivered. It was still quite cold.

High time that sun put in an appearance, else all would be lost! Francis grinned. The world was really a predictable place to live in. Augustine was right but wasnt right though obviously he wasnt wrong. He was a good strong man. If Francis had been like him he would have been quite happy.

The first bloke was looking at him. You'll do for me, he said.

What was that?

I said you'll do for me.

Francis nodded. Thanks. As long as you didnt take offence about that comment.

Och naw, fuck.

Francis nodded. And thanks for the drink.

Ye kidding? It's just a drink.

Aye well . . .

The bloke shrugged. That's how we were wanting to get a few bob, so's we could get a refill.

Mm, aye.

See your watch, we could get no bad for it.

Frank nodded. There was no chance, no fucking chance. Down by the fence the second bloke was gazing at him and he shifted on his seat immediately so that when he was looking straight ahead he was looking away from the three men. He didnt want to see them at the moment. There was something about them that was frightening. He was recognizing in

himself fear. He was scared, he was frightened; it was
the three men who were frightening him, something
in them together that was making him scared, the
sum of the parts, it was an evil force. If he just stared
straight ahead. If he stayed calm. He was on a bench
in the park and it was 10 a.m. There was a jogger
somewhere. All it needed was somebody to touch
him perhaps. If that happened he would die. His
heart would stop beating. If that happened he would
die and revelation. But if he just got up. If he was to
just get up off of the bench and start walking slowly
and deliberately along in the opposite direction, to
from where they had come. That would be fine if he
could just do that. But he couldnt, he couldnt do it;
his hands gripped his kneecaps, the knuckles pure
white. Did he want to die? What had his life been
like? Had it been worth living? His boyhood, what
like was his boyhood? had that been okay? It hadnt
been too bad he hadnt been too bad, he'd just been
okay normal, normal, the same as anybody else.
He'd just fallen into bad ways. But he wasnt evil.
Nobody could call him evil. He was not evil. He was
just an ordinary person who was on hard times who
was not doing as well as he used to and who would be
getting better soon once things picked up, he would
be fine again and able to be just the same, he was all
right, he was fine, it was just to be staring ahead.

In with the doctor

BY ONE OF those all-time flukes I landed head of the queue at the doctor's surgery. Somebody nudged me on the elbow eventually and pointed to the wee green light above the door. I laid down the magazine and walked across. The doctor opened it and said, You first this morning?

Yes sir, I says.

Yes sir! It was really incredible I could have said such a thing; I dont think I've called anybody sir in years. But the doctor took it in his stride, as if it was normal procedure; he ushered me inside, waiting to shut the door behind me. Then he walked side by side with me, leaving me at the patient's chair while he continued on round the desk to sit on his own one. He was quite a worried looking wee guy and it occurred to me he probably liked the drink too much. His face scarlet and his hair was prematurely white. He had on a white dustcoat, the kind hospital orderlies usually wear, but underneath it he was wearing an expensive three-piece suit. He sat watching me and frowned.

What's up? I says.

Aw nothing, nothing at all. Fancy a coffee?

Aye, ta, that'd be great. I sniffed and looked at the carpet while he rose to fill an electric kettle across at the sink. When he noticed me glance over he nodded. Aye, he says, this job, it's worse than you think. He grinned suddenly, he reached to plug in the kettle, then returned to the chair. I was reading that yin of Kafka's last night, 'The Country Doctor' – you read it?

Eh aye, I says.

Gives me the fucking willies... He shook his head: What about yourself?

Well, naw, no really.

It doesnt bother you!

Eh, no really.

He smiled. In this job you sometimes fall into the trap of thinking everybody's a doctor.

Pardon?

Naw, he says, you start talking to folk as if they're doctors.

Aw aye.

He frowned and turned to gaze at the electric kettle, he began muttering unintelligibly. Then he says, Probably I stuck in too much water and jammed the fucking thing! He shook his head and sighed loudly but it sounded a wee bit false. He got up off his seat and went to the window, he raised it and put his head out, and he whistled: Whsshhle whhssht!

The next thing the young lassie who works in the snackbar appeared. Her name was Brenda and she was roundabout 18, 19. Blonde-haired, but sometimes a bit sharp-tongued for my liking. He says to her, A piece on sausage hen, and a cup of coffee. Then he glanced at me: What about yourself?

Naw, no thanks.

He shrugged. Hey I hope it's ready the now Brenda!

Aye it's ready the now! she says.

Ah you're a lifesaver, a lifesaver!

So they tell me, she says.

He left the window ajar while she was away. The snackbar was parked permanently in the waste ground next to the surgery and it wasnt long till she reappeared. When she gives him the stuff she says, You can hand me the money in later on.

Aye alright.

I could hardly believe my ears. And I was thinking to myself, Aye ya bastard! if you werent a doctor! Frankly, I was beginning to get annoyed. Here he was having a teabreak and ben the room a pile of folk was sitting there waiting. And then another thing started annoying me as well. How come he was taking me into his confidence like this? At best it seemed as if he was making a hell of a lot of assumptions about me, and I didnt like it very much.

The kettle started boiling. He says to me: You sure you dont fancy a coffee?

Positive. Look eh I'm in cause of my back . . .

He nodded; he sniffed, then he took a bite of his piece. What is it sore? he says.

Sore? I says, It's fucking killing me!

Hh! He continued chewing the food, gazing at me occasionally; he was waiting for me to say something else. I shrugged: I think maybe it's caused by the damp.

He nodded. His attention wandered to the window then he sat to the front and glanced upwards and sideways, and indicated a framed certificate hanging on the wall. I was a mature student at Uni, he says. And he fingered the lapels of his dustcoat. I came late to this... I started only about three years ago. He shook his head and sighed. Ah Christ, it has to be said; to a fairly big extent you've got to describe this as a young man's job.

Mmm.

Aye, he says, truly, a young man's job.

Well, right enough, it needs a lot of training.

Naw but it's no just that. He grimaced at me and stared at his piece; he bit a mouthful and chewed,

then drank a mouthful of coffee. He sighed again
and he says: You married?

Eh, yes and no.

Separated?

I shrugged.

Ah – same as myself, I'm divorced. Hh! He
smiled: Up at Uni I got involved with this lassie
and *she* found out, the missis. Bang – out the
door. More or less dumped the fucking suitcase
out in the middle of the street man fucking terrible.
Never seen her since! No even at all these family
kind of business things. It's funny, when I dont
go to one she does and when I do go to one
she doesnt. And we never get in touch before-
hand. It's a kind of telepathy or some fucking
thing! He grinned at me: This auld uncle of mine,
having a laugh with me, he says he never knows
whether he's coming or going, is he going to see
me or is he going to see her! Makes him dizzy
he says!

I nodded.

Then there's the weans.

Aw. Aye.

You know what I'm talking about?

Aye.

Two I've got; how about yourself?

Four.

Four! Christ, aye, you do know what I'm talking about!

I shrugged.

But my two, he says, my two – aye, they're fine,
they're alright. He began chuckling: Aye, they're
alright.

I nodded.

Nice weans. I miss no seeing them. He frowned
suddenly and leaned forwards. What was I talking
about there?

Eh . . .

He carried on staring at me, waiting for me to
remember. To be honest, I was kidding on I didnt
know because I was hoping if he never found out he
would get ahead with the job in hand. But he started
getting fucking really strained and you could see he
was really intent on finding out so I says: Look eh,
I think it was something to do with women.

Aw aye Christ aye so it was. He nodded... Naw,
I was just going to say, this job man, the way you
feel at the end of the day it's well nigh fucking
impossible I mean if you're wanting to meet the
fair sex. You're just – you're knackered, simple
as that; you just dont want to go out anywhere.
I mean I've got this colleague and he was telling
me I should join one of these singles clubs. What
he was saying, he was saying it would just save all

the sweat of that initial carry on, the introductions and so forth.

He paused there, looking at me, awaiting my reaction. Then he says: I'm no sure but, to be honest, whether I fancy the idea. You hear these stories . . .

And he paused again, watching me. Eventually I nodded.

Okay, he says, so it's your back.

Well aye, sometimes it gets really achy.

Mmm . . . aches and pains, aches and pains . . . He lapsed into the sort of silence that lets you see he was miles away. There was one wee bit of bread left on his serviette and his fingers just picked it up and let it fall, picked it up and let it fall. Then he snorted and shook his head, he smiled at me: Kafka! From what I hear he was setting out to write this straightforward Chekov type doctor yarn. And what happens! Naw, he laughed briefly. I've had my bellyful of country fucking doctors!

Mm.

Aye, Christ, I was down in Galloway for a bit of my time, the training and so on. And I'll tell you something man I dont want to see another blade of grass. It was funny at first, all the gossip and the rest of it; then after a while you got used to it. Used to it! And I mean once you're fucking used to it you're...! Hh!

He shook his head and pursed his lips, dabbed at his mouth with the serviette, swallowed the last of his coffee. He gestured at the door: Many waiting?

Eh, quite a few. There might be more now right enough.

He sighed. To tell you straight, he says, they deserve better than me.

I watched him when he said it but he seemed to have spoken without any trace of irony whatsoever so I decided to reply in the same way. Look, I says, it isnt that so much; what it is, I think, really, is just that you dont seem to have the interest, I mean no really, no the way you should.

Mmm.

Well, you dont – Christ!

Naw you're right, I know. He glanced at the electric kettle. Think I'll have another coffee. What about yourself?

Eh aye, okay, fine.

Good. Heh I mean if you want a piece or something . . . ? He indicated the window.

Naw, I says, it's no that long since I ate my breakfast.

I mean hh! He shook his head and laughed briefly, gazed away over my head to someplace, one hand balanced on the handle of the kettle and the other in his dustcoat pocket. To be frank with you, I only

went to Uni to get involved in the ideas, metaphysics
and so on, the history of the intellect, the past and
the future and – aw Christ, fuck knows what else,
no point talking, no point talking. Them out there
in that waiting room man I mean, really, they dont
understand, they dont, they dont understand. And
it's no fucking for me to tell them, is it!

He patted himself on the chest to emphasise the
point, then he came walking back round to sit down
on his chair facing me. I nodded in reply to him but
I was non-committal; there was a certain amount of
elitism showing in his talk and I didnt appreciate it,
not one little bit. And no just the thing itself but the
way he was lumping me in the same boat as him.
I felt like saying: What about them ben there man
they're fucking sitting suffering!

And me and that lassie too, he was saying, me and
that lassie. No kidding ye man we were just really
interested in yapping on the gether – about all sorts
of things, Kepler and Copernicus, and auld fucking
Tycho! and we were relating it all to the painters of
the period. Really interesting I mean, really. I was
enjoying it Christ I've got to admit it. But that's
how I fucking went there in the first place I mean –
hh! Hey... He frowned at me: You ever read that
History of the Conflict Between Religion and Science
by John William Draper?

Eh aye, aye.

Well I'll tell you something for nothing, I think that's a great book... And he jabbed his finger at me as if his suspicions had been confirmed but he was still saying it anyway and I could go and take a fuck to myself.

I didnt respond except to nod vaguely. But I kept my gaze matching his. After a few moments there was a rap at the door and he went to answer it immediately. He was scowling. He said loudly: Yes?

Eh, I was just wanting that prescription renewed... It was a male voice.

Mm yes yes, yes, well I'm busy the now so you'll just have to wait your turn like everybody else.

Then he closed the door. He paused there for a wee while. And then he went over to the kettle and began examining it. He had forgotten to switch it on. This is why it hadnt boiled. He reached to the switch in such a way that I knew he was trying not to let me see. He gazed up at a pictorial calendar on the wall. After a moment he turned to me: You know something, he says, a few of them still act surprised because I'm weer than the average.

Honest?

Aye, he says, smiling.

Well, I suppose that's because they're used to doctors being this and that, because they've got certain expectations about what doctors should and should not be.

Exactly. Aye. They think doctors're like the fucking polis, you've got to be 6 feet tall to get in!

I laughed with him. I says, Aye but it's probably a class thing.

Probably, aye. He frowned and glanced back at the electric kettle. Then he sniffed. What d'you work at yourself?

I'm on the broo the now.

Aw are you!

Nearly eighteen month.

What! Jesus Christ! And he stared at me, a frown beginning to appear on his face.

What's up? I says.

Pardon?

Naw I mean how come you're so surprised? Is it because I've read cunts like Kafka and John William Draper?

Naw naw, not at all, not at all.

I didnt believe him.

Naw, he says again, not at all, not at all, it's no that. It's your suit.

My suit! You kidding?

Naw, I mean, the cloth.

Ah well, aye, but I mean it's an auld yin man Christ I mean... There's a lot of cunts walking about with better yins than this and they're on the broo as well.

So?

So! What d'you mean fucking so?

He stared at me.

Your fucking inference, I says after a few moments, it shows you're no really in touch with what's going on.

He nodded and felt the kettle.

Look, I says, if you want to know what I really think... I think you're an elitist wee bastard – your attitudes.

My attitudes!

Aye your attitudes. Especially considering you were a mature student and the rest of it.

Hh! He shook his head at me, grinning sarcastically. Well, he says, that's a fucking good yin right enough. I mean dont tell me this is linked to that hoary auld fucking misconception that the vast majority of mature students are all good fucking socialists.

What?

A load of shite that – Christ, you want to have seen the cunts I met up there! He made a face at me then laughed briefly: Tell me this, he says, how come you called me sir when you walked in that door? Was it because I'm a doctor?

Naw it wasnt because you were a doctor.

Are you sure?

Naw I'm no fucking sure.

Ah.

Well how can I be I mean Christ – anyway, I was trying to figure that yin out myself, earlier on. And I dont know, I dont honestly know. I was figuring it was because you're a doctor but that cant be right cause I've met stacks of yous in my time, stacks of yous. I mean I *never* call any cunt sir!

Mm... The kettle began to boil at long last but he just switched it off and came back round to sit down on his chair, he was frowning at something and he looked at me, then smiled: Okay, he says, these folk ben the waiting room there, I dont see you rushing to let them in.

Pardon?

I said I dont see you rushing to let them in.

Aw well that's no fair, that's just no fair. Fuck sake I mean you've no even seen me yet!

Mmm... He nodded. Sore back you said?

Aye, sore back. And it's fucking genuine and all so it is.

I didnt say it wasnt.

Naw, I know, but look it really is sore I mean . . .

Okay, he says, sorry. I apologise – for the wee dig and that.

Ah well. I shrugged. Aye and fair enough, I says, I'm sitting here chatting to you when there's a lot of folk waiting to be seen and eh... There again but, maybe that's cause you're a doctor after all, relating it for instance to the way I said sir.

Expectations – aye, you're right, what a doctor should and should not be. That was one of the things in *The Country Doctor* I thought Kafka got terrific.

Pardon?

Ah, sorry, sorry, you'll no really know.

I nodded. Then I says, But what I was meaning there was you, being the doctor, holding the position of power, you've got to dismiss me, else I'll wind up being here for the rest of my days!

He laughed and stood up and came round to me. Just open your jacket, he says, and pull your shirt out your trousers, and your vest if you've got one on.

I did as he said and I also leaned forwards a little so's he could see properly. He used a stethoscope, and then began tapping about with something that felt like a steel mallet; and it was quite bloody sore when he kept it tapping on the same spot. Then he says, Have you got a lumpy mattress?

Even though I couldnt see his face I knew he

must have been smiling, that he had been cracking a wee joke. And he says: Naw, I dont want to disappoint you!

I didnt say anything back for a minute. There was no point losing my temper. I heard him sniff and he began putting the stethoscope higher up my spine. Breathe in, he says.

I did as he told me a couple of times and when he'd finished I says: Look, believe it or not, it is genuine; I did come in here to find out if there was anything up with my back.

Aw I know, I know, it's just... He came round from behind me and put the stethoscope on the side of the desk. In my experience there's a lot of folk love to get told bad news about their health, it means they can lie down and die in peace, without being bothered by any cunt.

Pardon?

He only smiled in answer.

Naw, what d'you say there?

He shook his head but was still smiling. It was a really smug kind of smile and I didnt like it one little bit. I'll tell you something, I says, you're a smug wee bastard. I dont like the way you think you understand all.

Ah I know. He nodded. It is a bad habit I've picked up. He yawned and stuck his hands into his trouser pockets and he strolled to the window, swaggering slightly; and he gazed out for some time. Then he glanced round at me and squinted at his wristwatch. It's a digital, he says, you cant always see what time it is. Fucking useless as far as I'm concerned.

He continued looking at me; till it dawned on me what he was after. O pardon me, I says, you've finished.

Aye... He yawned again and turned back to the window.

I was actually out the door before I realised the fucking situation, crossing the floor to the exit, tucking in my vest and shirt. Hey wait a minute, I says to myself, you're no letting the cunt away with that are you? Back I went – and I was feeling as fucking annoyed as ever I did in a long time. He was standing there just inside his doorway, ushering in the next patient. Hey you, I says, wait a wee minute, I've got something to say.

You've missed your turn, he whispers.

I have not missed my turn.

Aye you have.

Naw I've no. You dismissed me before I was ready, playing your wee class games.

I was not playing any wee class games.

Aye you were.

I was not. He frowned at me and then he glared to the side of where I was standing, as though he had spotted folk trying to peer in from the waiting-room.

And the other person who was to go in to see him said: Eh doctor, excuse me . . .

The doctor shook his head. Sorry, he says, sorry, you'll just need to... And he grabbed me by the wrist and took me inside, shutting the door.

I removed his hand.

He was already halfway round to his seat. Okay, he was saying, I've got no time for this sort of carry on. Just state your problem.

There isnt any problem. There's just facts, facts – statements of fact.

He nodded. He placed his elbow on the edge of his desk and dropped his chin to rest on the palm of his hand.

Okay, I says, it's all hell of a fucking boring, I know, I know. But what I really object to is the way you've made your assumptions about me, about what I am and what I believe man that's what I fucking object to, all these assumptions. But leave that aside; it's the way you've acted, no like a doctor at all. Christ sake I mean I shouldnt've had to sit here listening to all that crap when these poor cunts ben the waiting-room are getting ignored, and for all you know are literally dying – literally, dying!

He smiled and raised his head, straightened his shoulders and clasped his hands on the desk. Well, he says, you're letting me down now. I didnt expect you to come away with a chestnut like that for fuck sake I mean we're all literally dying.

Aw aye, very good.

Naw but... He grinned. I truly believed you had a genuine interest in the whys and wherefores of this game, that's how I've been yapping on. I mean... He leaned forwards: D'you think I go about offering every cunt a coffee?

You've no even fucking gave me it yet!

He frowned slightly.

I mean you offered me one two or three times but you never got round to actually fucking giving me it.

O, sorry.

It doesnt matter I mean I was only fucking taking it for politeness man Christ I wasnt even really bothered. Anyhow, I dont want this to detract from my main point and that is you, lumping me in the same boat as yourself. As far as I'm concerned you're an elitist wee shite and I fucking resent getting linked to you, to your beliefs. Okay? And the sooner we get a new doctor here the better.

Aye, and so say all of us.

Ah well you would say that wouldnt ye.

Maybe. He shrugged. It doesnt mean it's no the case. Actually I only came back to this city out a sense of duty. I hate the fucking dump to be perfectly frank about it. It was some sort of filial obligation, I wanted to impress my father – and he's fucking dead! That's the joke!

Pardon? What d'you mean?

He was dead. I was wanting to impress him and he was dead. How do you impress somebody that's dead?

You mean you knew he was dead like?

Aye. Just – one of these daft things you do. Too many fucking Hollywood movies! Naw, Christ... He got up and strolled to the window. Take a look out there, he says, it's a fucking disgrace. Here I am trying to run a doctor's surgery and I can hardly get fucking moving for dirt and dust and dods of garbage man blowing in the fucking door every time it gets opened for something I mean Christ sake man you're talking about that lot ben there!

And he was gesticulating at the door now with his voice raised quite high: Just tell me this, how come they dont go out there and build a fucking barricade!

What?

A barricade. They could fucking erect a barricade man to stop all the garbage blowing in the door.

I stared at him, then added: You should go and join BUPA ya cunt!

Aw thanks, thanks a lot.

Well no wonder.

Hh! He smiled. You know something? Chekov didnt even practise medicine; I mean no really.

Aye he did.

Naw he never!

He fucking did.

He didnt, I'm telling you, no really. I mean I dont even envy him because he was a brilliant writer I just fucking envy him because he got engrossed in ideas.

I dont believe you.

You ever counted up the number of doctors who became writers and artists, and musicians? Well there's been a hell of a lot, a hell of a lot.

Okay, fine, so you think it's better being one of them than the poor cunt who has to go about curing the sick.

He was about to reply but stopped himself and he says instead: The question doesnt even interest me. At one time it did but no now, no any longer. The way I see it I have to survive as best I can and sometimes that's bound to mean doing things that upset cunts like you.

Things like sitting about gabbing when you've a waiting-room stowed out with patients.

Pardon?

You – when people're waiting to see you man you dont even fucking bother acknowledging them hardly, their existence, you dont even bother, you're quite happy just sitting here fucking complaining to me.

Who's complaining?

You are ya cunt ye. Since I came in here, you've done nothing else. You hate your job and you hate the surgery and you hate the fucking city and you wish you could spend the rest of your days just farting about gabbing like a bourgeois fucking intellectual. Well I'll tell you something, I think you've got a big chip on your shoulder and that's it, end of story.

Aw thanks, thanks a lot.

Naw, no kidding but, you're wee – at least, weer than the average – and you're a bit older than your contemporaries, the ones you went to Uni with. And you wear the wrong clothes and you drink too fucking much and your hair's prematurely white. And your wife's fucking threw you out the house for messing about with a lassie and you dont get seeing the weans as much as you'd like. And aye, also, from what I read into the situation, your sex life is nil, absolutely nil.

I stopped there but I continued looking at him. I

felt it was necessary to do this because I also felt I had gone over the score in what I had said to him. But I couldnt take anything back. It was said, and that was that.

He smiled, then he put his right hand up to cover his face, as if he was trying not to break down in front of me. In fact it wasnt that at all. He looked at me very seriously and he says, I doubt if you've truly understood a single thing I've said.

Hh – well I think the very opposite. I think I understand only too well, only too fucking well.

Aw well then there's nothing more to be said.

Exactly.

If you would just tell the next patient to come ben on your way out . . .

Naw, will I fuck, do it yourself.

He smiled. I knew you'd say that, this is why I said it; in fact I've got a wee light I switch on, so you dont have to say fuck all – okay?

Aye, aye, great, that's great with me.

Good, glad to hear it... He nodded then sniffed and glanced down at his desk.

After a moment I says: So what've you dismissed me or what? It's hard to tell.

He looked at me in an odd way, and I knew it was what to do next was the problem.